CASCADE

by T. J. Fox

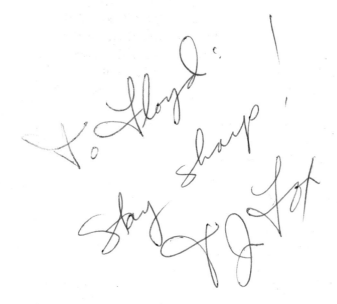

International Standard Book Number: 1-55666-033-2
Library of Congress Catalogue Card Number: 89-45151
Printed in the United States of America

Published in 1988 by
AUTHORS UNLIMITED
3330 Barham Blvd., #204
Los Angeles, CA 90068
(213) 874-0902

Dedicated
to
Linda
... an encouraging force
who allows me to see beyond
the limits others set.

Chapter 1

Justine traveled down the Bureau halls, with her usual bouncy confidence. Her dark hair floated around her face, as her heels clicked distinctively, against the polished floors. Like sunlight on a country pond, her dark eyes danced and glinted as she bade good morning to her associates. Justine had an inherent way of making others smile, despite themselves. Her good natured optimism could be contagious at times. The smartly tailored blue suit she wore this morning was indicative of her dress for success attitude. She made a concerted effort to be stylish, up to date, and always... just so.

Justine's work with the Bureau had, to date, been routine, minor cases. Her good looks, instead of helping her advance, had actually been holding her back. Though her work was well above average, higher-ups feared the "got the promotion because of her looks" gossip, so they overcompensated. They kept passing her over for the bigger assignments. Time and time again, the less proficient, less attractive women, in her department, moved up and onward. It was becoming a source of desperation for Justine. She had all but resolved herself, to confront her superiors with her dissatisfaction.

With a physically obvious let down, Justine stepped into her small office, closing the door behind her. She hung her jacket and flipped the lid from her cafeteria coffee. Somewhat distracted, she sat at her desk and glanced through the mail. Surprise, then pleasure crossed her face as she read the confidential memo.

DATE: April 11

TO: Blake Hampton

         Justine Edwards

FROM: Harold Compson

SUBJECT: .... Preston Montgomery

> Please be in my office, 9:00 am, this date, to discuss above subject.

Justine wanted to jump up and down and scream but she managed, just barely, to maintain a modicum of propriety. She tried to concentrate on the paperwork from the last completed case, but found her mind jumping back to the memo. The clock clicked off the minutes ever so slowly. Finally, 10 minutes to 9 rolled over on the digital. Justine nearly exploded from her chair, regained her composure, then stepped out into the hall. Quickly she moved toward the elevator, colliding with her superior, Blake Hampton.

"Oh, excuse me." Justine was embarrassed.

"Perfectly all right." Blake was his usual cool self.

Everything had been strictly business between Blake and Justine, although Justine had, on occasion, dreamt about the possibility of more. Blake was of medium height and build, with cool green eyes and sandy blonde hair...a fashionable dresser like Justine; always... just so. Being quiet and keeping to himself outside of the office, caused much speculation about his private life. No one had any solid information. But then, few people in the office knew much about Justine either. Since her move to Washington, she'd devoted her time almost solely to her job. She had no social life to speak of; not that she wasn't pursued. She just didn't feel she had the time to attempt a relationship. Her career was her focus. Maybe it was the same with Blake.

Justine and Blake were the only ones in the elevator to ascend to the top floor. Justine felt somewhat awkward, alone with Blake in this small space. Blake showed no sign of any difficulties. He showed little sign that he was even aware of her presence. Security on the top floor was tighter than anywhere in the building. Guards checked ID's right at the elevator and then again, before entry to the offices. Mr. Compson's office was ominous... dark draperies, heavy furniture, and the smell of leather in the air. Justine wasn't quite sure if the leathered fragrance came from the furniture or Mr. Compson's aftershave. Mr. Compson didn't look up, but motioned them to sit. Sitting on the edge of the chair, Justine anxiously waited for the bearish man behind the desk to speak. Finally, Mr. Compson cleared his throat and looked at them, over his reading glasses.

"Blake, Gilbro has all the files on the Montgomery cases. He'll give them to you, when we're finished here. Briefly, we have reason to believe that Mr. Montgomery has recently moved into a new field. To date, we had no reference to his dealing in drugs. However, some sketchy information was received from one of our operatives in the Northeast a few days ago. Montgomery's name has come up in connection with a large shipment of cocaine. We are not sure if the cocaine has arrived or is arriving. We need to put someone on the inside."

Blake's eyes narrowed, as he leaned forward in his chair. "And who did you have in mind?"

Mr. Compson raised his eyebrows in a sense of disbelief at Blake's lack of perception. "Ms. Edwards, of course."

"I see." Blake leaned back in his chair and folded his arms across his chest.

"We have 'arranged' for Mr. Montgomery's personal assistant to... take a leave. So he will be looking for a temporary replacement." Mr. Compson handed Justine a file. "Here is a copy of the application we will forward to Mr.

3

Montgomery, along with several references that he will find more than satisfactory. All your background information is in there, as well. Mr. Montgomery is not stupid or we'd have nailed him by now. So, make sure you know your cover. He'll test you and he'll try to trap you, with your own words. Choose them carefully. I am confident, Ms. Edwards, that you will handle this assignment in the same adept and thorough manner as you have every case thus far assigned to you. You are undoubtedly wondering just why you were chosen for this assignment?"

Justine nodded.

"Our first consideration was your earlier work experience, as a secretary and personal assistant. Your work record in that field was equally as exemplary as it is here. Second, you are an attractive woman. Montgomery can afford to be choosy, so you need as many pluses as you can get."

Mr. Compson turned to Blake. "Blake, I want you, personally, on the outside for this one. We want this man and we don't want any screw-ups. You and Ms. Edwards go over the material and set yourselves up. When you're ready, give the word and we'll start the ball rolling."

"Is there an alternate plan, if she can't get inside?" Blake looked hopeful.

Mr. Compson smiled at Justine. "She'll get in. That's all." Mr. Compson waved his hand indicating the meeting was over.

Justine got up and shook Mr. Compson's hand, thanking him for giving her the assignment. When she left, Blake was still sitting.

Blake waited, til the door closed, to speak. He leaned forward in his chair, again. "Harold, are you crazy?"

"No... at least, I don't think so."

"You can't put her that close to him."

"And why not?"

"You know why not. It's too dangerous. You didn't tell her everything. And she's exactly the type he picks on."

"Justine is a professional."

"She's never had an assignment even close to being as dangerous as this one."

4

"Everyone has a first big case. You did... and not all that long ago. Besides, you'll be on the outside to make sure nothing goes wrong."

"I don't think she's ready."

"I do. And since I'm the boss, I guess... I win."

Blake started to leave. "Oh, and Blake... don't try to sabotage this. I want her in and you do what you have to, to get her in. That's an order."

Obviously upset, Blake left the office, slamming the door. He stood a moment, outside the office; cooled his anger... an anger that came, from some strange unknown place inside him; then went to Gilbro's office for the files. Plunking himself down in the chair beside Gilbro's desk, Blake spoke bluntly. "Harold said you have the Montgomery files for me."

"Right here." Gilbro handed Blake a one foot stack of files.

"This everything?"

"Everything from the file room I could find."

Blake eyed Gilbro, suspiciously, then began skimming through the files. He reached the last folder and, still, hadn't found what he was seeking. "All right, Gilbro, where is it?"

"Where's what?"

"Gilbro... I worked a file on Montgomery before... the sex slaying we couldn't nail him on. Where is it?"

"Gee, I don't know. If it was in the file room and someone had it out, there should have been a red card in its place. There wasn't any red card."

Blake ground his teeth and tightened his jaw. He was having unusual difficulty keeping his temper under control. "Look, you tell Harold that I want that file. I'm not going to let her get close to Montgomery, unless she knows everything. In order for an agent to do his job properly, he must have all the facts, not just some of them. Tell him I want the file, before the end of the day."

"OK, I'll tell him." Gilbro knew Blake well enough not to argue with him.

Blake collected the armload of material and carried it back to his office. He let it sit in a heap on the corner of his

5

desk until late that afternoon, when Gilbro arrived with the missing file. The two men exchanged knowing glances and Gilbro shrugged his shoulders. "What can I say?"

Blake half smiled, "Get out of here."

Gilbro left.

Blake fingered the file a moment, before opening it. Once opened, the file brought back vivid memories of a dead end investigation. Montgomery had a passion for attractive young women, thus his involvement with pornography. His interest in these women was sometimes sadistic, and in this particular case, deadly. They hadn't been able to successfully link Montgomery with the brutal slaying, so he was never charged. Blake remembered seeing the body of that young woman. The terror and pain in her eyes haunted him, long after he left the case. It was still an open file. Blake didn't like the idea of a woman... especially someone he knew, being within arms length of Montgomery. All the investigations and interviews that had been done on the case pointed toward the fact that every woman who had actually gone under Montgomery's hand was 25 to 35, shapely, dark haired, dark eyed and fair complected... a perfect match with Justine. Blake closed the file and hit the desk with his fist. "Damn you, Harold. You picked her because you know he'll go for her. Damn you... for being right."

Justine sat, impatient, in her office, waiting for Blake to call her to his office. She skipped lunch, so not to miss the call. Four o'clock rolled over on the digital and the phone rang almost simultaneously. Justine jumped at the sound, then answered anxiously.

"Ms. Edwards... Can you work late?"

"Yes."

"Then come over to my office and we'll start working on this project. I'll arrange to have dinner sent in."

"Yes, sir."

Justine grabbed a note pad, the file Mr. Compson had given her, and a pen. She dashed out the door, arriving at Blake's office, slightly out of breath. Blake glanced up at her, as she entered the room.

"Have a seat. First we'll go over the background on Montgomery, then over your cover background. After that, we'll work out a plan of operation."

Blake was very businesslike and very professional. He opened the first file, then the next, and the next, until the previously missing file was the only one left.

"Let's break for dinner. Do you like Chinese?"

"That's fine." Justine would have preferred Mexican or Italian.

"Great." Blake placed the order, then excused himself from the office. Justine glanced up at the clock... 7:30. Wearily, she got up, stretched and went to the window. Thoughtfully, she looked out onto the night city. Many ideas crowded her mind. Her first big case. This Montgomery had his finger in many pies. He was indeed a clever man, to have thwarted the Bureau for so many years. He would be a real prize. Smiling to herself, she thought back on Mr. Compson complimenting her capabilities... and her looks. His words had pumped new life into her deflated morale.

Blake waited in the lobby for the dinner delivery. He stood near the guard's desk. "Hey Pete, what's up?"

"Not much, Mr. Hampton. I haven't seen you here this late for a while."

"Lot of work to do today... Ms. Edwards is here too. Do me a favor?"

"Sure."

"I'm going to send her home in a couple hours. Make sure one of the guards takes her to her car, OK?"

"Sure thing, Mr. Hampton."

The boy from the restaurant appeared at the glass doors. Smiling, the guard unlocked the door and let him inside. Blake paid the boy, giving him a handsome tip, and took the food. Then the guard relocked the door. Blake went to the elevator. "See ya later, Pete."

The guard nodded and went back to his desk.

Justine was still staring out the window when Blake returned. Blake sneered at the sprawl of paper on his desk. "Let's go eat in the conference room."

Justine followed him. The food smelled good and looked as good as it smelled. Justine tasted the sweet and sour pork. "Mmmm. This is delicious."

"Yeah, the Wang Chow Restaurant has excellent food. I use them a lot." A long pause ensued, then Blake broke in, quietly. "You sure you want to do this?"

Justine was surprised by the question. "You mean the assignment?"

"Yes."

"Yes. I'm sure I want to do the job."

Blake nodded and went back to his dinner. Neither spoke again, until they'd finished eating. Blake tossed the empty containers into the trash. "Ready to go back to work?"

Justine nodded and followed him back to the office. She felt like a puppy following after the "big dog".

Blake sat, then took a deep breath. "Now, I have to warn you. This next file is somewhat... gruesome. Here. You read it over, then we'll discuss it... if you have any questions."

Blake handed Justine the file and watched her face for expression. She showed no emotion, as she read, until she flipped to the pictures of the dead woman. Justine wished she hadn't just eaten. She wanted to be sick, but somehow sensed that this was a test of her ability to remain detached. She turned the page and fought down the nausea. She read through the interviews and summaries, then closed the file and handed it back to Blake. She understood now, just why she'd been chosen. She sat back in her chair and looked Blake straight in the eye. Blake's eyes steeled on hers. "We never did identify her."

"Mr. Compson is well known for his ability to pick just the right agent for an undercover assignment. He may have outdone himself this time. The setup may be too perfect."

"You want to back-off the assignment, then?" Blake looked hopeful.

"No, Mr. Hampton. I've finally, gotten a chance to prove myself and I'm not going to let go of it."

"Nothing will change your mind?"

"No."

Blake's face showed his disappointment, "Then let's set up the project. Montgomery is based in, of all places, a small town in Virginia called Wilson Falls. We'll need to set up a cover for me, so I can go down first. Real estate I think. Usually the only thing you can get by with in a small town. I'll go down there, looking to buy some land. I'll use the name Blake Parrum."

Blake wrote as he spoke. "We'll need a code name for the project. Any ideas?"

Justine thought... Wilson Falls... Falls... "Cascade".

"Yeah, that's good. I like it. Project Cascade. Now, get out your background file. Your name is Justine Price... simple and easy to remember. You can memorize all the background info in say, 3 days can't you?"

Justine nodded, as she took notes.

"We'll set up the usual telephone recording as one of your outside access capabilities. Of course, if you can't use the phone, you'll need the coded beeper. They gave you one on that Hastings assignment didn't they?"

"Yes."

"Then they've already explained it to you..." There was a long pause. "... One thing I want to make very clear... if you get into trouble, even if you only suspect they might have made you, you get out! Understood?"

"Yes." Justine was convinced Blake didn't think she could handle this assignment and resolved she'd make this case... any way she could.

"That's enough for tonight. Take two days out of the office. Stay home and work on your background. Come in on Thursday, ready to be tested and work out the kinks. Good night, Ms. Edwards."

Justine took one last side glance at Blake on her way out. He looked unusually tired and tense, not things she had occasion to see in him. He was always so cool and confident... so totally "in control". She couldn't help wondering if maybe that last file hadn't upset him a little as well.

Chapter 2

Next morning, Justine was surprised to find her brother Steve on her doorstep. Steve was the only family Justine had left. He looked handsome in his military uniform. "Steve!" Justine threw her arms around him and hugged him tightly. "What are you doing here? Why didn't you tell me you were coming?"

"Can I come in?"

"Oh," Justine laughed giddily, "Yes, yes, come inside."

Steve dropped his bags inside the door and slipped out of his jacket, plopping himself down on the couch. "Feels good to relax."

"Well... What's going on?"

"Oh, you want to know what's going on?"

"Yes... yes, tell me... now... or else." Justine put on a threatening face.

"As of tomorrow morning I am a civilian again."

Justine was taken back. "You didn't reup?"

"Nope."

"Well, I am surprised. But, if that's what you want, I'm glad for you. What are you going to do?"

"If it's all right with you, I'd like to stay with you awhile... while I'm looking for a job."

"Sure, as long as you want."

"Sis, I have to ask you something." Steve looked serious.

"Yes?" Justine looked equally serious.

"Will you make me some breakfast? I'm starved."

"You idiot..." Justine threw a pillow at him. "... How do you want your eggs?"

"Over easy, two strips of bacon, a couple hot cakes, maybe a blueberry muffin, some French toast, fresh squeezed orange juice, coffee black, and a big glass of fresh milk."

"All right, all right. I'll get dressed and we'll go out for breakfast. But I have to get right back here. I have work to do."

As the Sanford had the best breakfasts in town, they went there. Steve was too busy stuffing himself to talk much. The first actual words to pass his lips, came only after his plate was empty. "So, sis, what's the big case you're working on, now? Someone stealing pens again at the Pentagon?"

"Very funny. As a matter of fact, I've just been given my first big assignment."

"Oh yeah? What is it?"

"I can't tell you."

"Aw, come on."

"Nope." Justine was smug.

"Just for that... I'm going to let you pay for breakfast." Steve left her with the check and waited outside.

Back at the apartment, Steve took a nap and Justine poured over her background information. She had to be perfect. She had to show Blake Hampton he was wrong. It was after 5, when Steve crawled out of bed. "Gee, I was really zonked. What's for dinner?"

"You tell me."

"Let's go out..."

"Where we going?"

"Someplace Chinese?"

"Oh, no... I had Chinese last night."

"I'm buying and I want Chinese."

Justine sighed to herself and flipped the file closed. "What is it men have about Chinese food?"

"Makes us virile!"

Justine laughed. "Alright, I had food from Wang Chow's last night. It was very good. We can go there... if you're sure you're buying."

"I'm buying, I'm buying."

Steve and Justine had always been affectionate toward each other... lots of hugs and physical contact. Steve was quite a bit taller than Justine and he liked to walk with his arm over her shoulders. That's how they entered Wang Chow's. Justine was so caught up in Steve's jubilation at being out and all the anecdotes he'd collected, that she failed to notice Blake Hampton sitting at the back of the restaurant. He watched them, but never made his presence known to Justine.

The sun was barely over the horizon, when the phone rang. Justine was in the shower and yelled to Steve to answer.

"Hello."

The voice on the line hesitated a moment. "... May I speak to Ms. Edwards?"

"Can she call you back? She's in the shower."

"Uh... yes. Ask her to call Blake Hampton. She has the number. Thank you." The phone clicked off.

Steve spoke to Justine through the bathroom door. "It was somebody named Blake Hampton."

Justine stepped out, wrapped in a towel. "My boss?"

"I guess. Said to call him. The guy sounds a little strange to me." Steve made a face. "I'm going to be out all day. I took your spare key. Don't wait up." Steve pecked Justine on the cheek.

"Have a good day, Steve. And Steve... I'm glad you're here. I've missed you." Steve just smiled.

Justine dressed and returned Blake's call. "Mr. Hampton, Justine Edwards. You phoned?"

"Yes... I'm sorry I called so early. I just wanted to see how it was going."

"It's going fine. I'll be ready by tomorrow."

"OK... well... I'll see you in the morning."

The phone clicked off and Justine looked quizzically at the receiver. "Strange..."

Blake plunked the receiver back into the cradle and turned his chair toward the window. Something peculiar was happening to him. He found anger, just below the surface, and it worried him. He couldn't be objective and clear-thinking with all this pent up hostility. Toward whom? For what? He checked himself out of the office, for the afternoon, and went to the shooting range. He unloaded cartridge after cartridge into the targets with a 100% kill rate. Yet, as he fired the last shot, he noted the hostility was still hanging onto him. Maybe it was the job, maybe it was the case, maybe it was...

After leaving the shooting range, Blake found himself driving around the city, going nowhere in particular. The car came to rest in a space across from Justine's apartment. His view into Justine's livingroom was unobstructed. Justine was sitting on the couch, papers spread out on the table. Justine's apartment had a private entrance. So, there was no mistake that the man going up the steps was going to see Justine. Blake watched, as the man entered the apartment with a bottle of wine. Though he could hear nothing, he watched intently.

Steve was in a celebrating mood. "Hey, sis. You still working? The work day is over. You're working too much. You need to have some fun. I brought some champagne to celebrate."

"No, Steve. I have to work on this."

"No ya don't. You've been working on it, since I got here. It's time for a break."

Steve flipped the open folders shut. Justine leaned back into the couch. "Well, where is my glass?"

Steve rushed to the kitchen and ran back with the glasses. He popped the cork and some of the champagne escaped the bottle, onto the files. "Oops!"

"Steve! You're going to get me in trouble."

"It'll dry! Here." Steve filled a glass and pushed it into her hand. "To my freedom."

They drank the toast. Steve poured, again. "To my big sister's big case." They drank. "To..."

"Steve! No! You're going to get me drunk."

"Loosen up a little, sis. You are entirely too serious, for as young and attractive as you are. Before you know it, you're going to be old and grey and wondering what happened." Steve put his arm around her and spoke softly. "Come on. Be happy with me. I love you... and I missed you too."

Justine couldn't help but give in to her baby brother's affectionate plea. "OK. Two more toasts and that's it."

"Agreed." Steve noticed the drapes standing open. "What are you doing sitting here, with the drapes open after dark. You know how many wierdos there are out there?"

"I forgot."

Steve shook his head. "What am I going to do with you?" With one swift motion, Steve closed the drapes. Blake sat a moment longer, then drove home.

The alarm met Justine's unwilling ears and she struggled to turn it off. With effort, she sat up on the edge of the bed, but had to lay back down to find her head. Steve burst into the room carrying a glass and speaking in a loud voice. "Gee, sis, I hope you don't drink when you're out on a date! By the end of the fourth toast you were passed out. Good thing I'm your brother."

"Don't yell, Steve."

"Hangover, huh?"

Steve sat on the side of the bed. "I'm sorry, sis. I shouldn't have made you drink so much. But you really must have been up-tight, to have gone out so easy. Here." Steve thrust the glass at her. "It'll help your head."

"How come you feel so good?"

"I'm used to a somewhat higher consumption of alcohol than you, my dear."

"My... my... don't we sound proper, this morning."

"Come on. Out of bed. Can't have you late for work. In the shower." Steve pushed Justine into the bath. As Justine showered and tried to stop the explosions in her head, Steve spoke to her from the bedroom. "Justine..."

"Yes?"

"I'll drive you to work, if you let me use your car today. I got a date."

Justine slipped out of the bathroom, her hair wrapped in a towel. "OK. But not like last time! You be there to pick me up at 5 sharp." Justine wagged her finger at Steve in a scolding manner.

"Yes, ma'am!" Steve saluted.

Steve dropped Justine at the entrance, and sped away. Before going to her office, Justine stopped in the ladies room. The eye drops had vanquished most of the redness in her eyes, but her face hurt, when she smiled. Even her hair seemed trying to pull itself out at the roots, adding to her discomfort. It had been a long time since she'd over indulged. Now, she was remembering why she didn't like to drink. Taking one last look at herself in the mirror, she could only hope no one would notice how awful she felt.

Blake Hampton was waiting in her office, staring out the window. Justine was startled to find him there. "Oh, good morning."

He didn't turn. "You're late."

Justine glanced at the clock as she hung her jacket. She was 2 minutes late. "I'm sorry.'"

"If you're going to take on a big assignment, you have to put a lot of time and effort into it."

"I understand that."

"You're telling me you're ready, then?"

"I believe so."

"Give me the file." Justine handed him the file. He jerked it from her hands and opened it. As luck would have it, the

16

first page he turned to was one wearing dried spots of spilled champagne. "What's happened to this?"

"I'm sorry. It got a little wet, but nothing was lost."

Blake threw the file on the desk and stormed from the office, yanking the door into its frame. Justine was completely at a loss over his behavior. His slamming the door hadn't helped her head any, either.

Blake's fit of temper carried him straight to Mr. Compson's office, where he invited himself to sit. "Harold, we have to talk."

Mr. Compson was calm, as always. "What must we talk about?"

"Ms. Edwards."

"What about her?"

"She can't handle this assignment."

"Why is that?"

"She's not taking it seriously. She's not doing her job."

"You and she went over her background and she wasn't ready? Is that what you're telling me?"

"Well... no... but she..."

"You didn't test her?"

Blake sighed and looked away. "No."

Mr. Compson picked up the phone. "Gilbro... Go down to Ms. Edward's office and check her out, on her background. She has the file... As soon as you're finished, report back to me."

Mr. Compson replaced the phone, folded his hands and spoke, again, to Blake. "Sit down Blake. What's going on with you?"

"I told you... she's not ready."

"We're going to find out. If Gilbro comes back with a negative report, I'll admit I was wrong. For now... I'll order some coffee and we'll wait for his report."

"No... I've got work to do." Blake got up to leave.

"Sit down Blake and wait." Mr. Compson was insistent.

Blake drank several cups of black coffee and paced the room, as they waited. Blankly, Blake was thumbing through a magazine when Gilbro entered the office. "Well, Gilbro?" Mr. Compson listened for the report.

"I ran the full gambit with her... twice and even threw in a few questions of my own."

"And?"

"She was a hundred percent."

"Thank you, Gilbro. That's all." The door clicked shut and a heavy silence hung in the air. Mr. Compson was first to speak, in an unexpected soft tone. "Blake, again, I ask you... What's going on?"

"Nothing."

"Blake, I'm getting the feeling there is something personal in this. It has no place here. If you can't get it under control you'll be the one I'll replace on this assignment. Work it out! Now get out of here!" Mr. Compson's tone had started out gentle, but ended in his usual bearish manner.

After taking a long walk, Blake returned to Justine's office. Justine was working busily at her desk. "Ms. Edwards..."

Justine looked up, inquiringly. "Yes, Mr. Hampton?"

"I apologize for my behavior, earlier. It was unprofessional... childish. I'd like to start the day over, if we may?"

"Of course." Justine was polite, yet cautious.

Blake closed the door. "If you'll give me the file, we'll go over a few things."

They spent the afternoon mulling through her cover, his cover, methods of contact, time schedules, transportation, etc. All the strings to pull the operation together were detailed. Blake's face showed severe emotional drain, as their meeting drew to a close. "I guess that covers everything, except your wardrobe. This operation requires an expensive look. Go see Mrs. Kirby, in purchasing. She'll give you a PO number and tell you which shops to use. Ask Mrs. Kelzo to take you. She'll know what's appropriate. Since you'll probably be busy all day tomorrow with that, I'll see about the transportation and tell Harold to get the ball rolling. Then we wait for the rat to take the bait."

Blake displayed an insincere and slightly embarrassed smile, upon leaving Justine's office. Justine wondered what problems he had that were boiling under the surface. They must be horrendous, to pierce through his perpetually cool exterior.

Chapter 3

All that was left was to wait. Wait for the call that would put the operation in motion. By the following Friday, Justine felt as if they had miscalculated and Montgomery rat that he was had smelled the poison in the bait. Finally, the call came through to the special phone in the switch room. The call was accepted and transferred to Justine. The red light on Justine's phone flashed, informing her that the call she'd been waiting for had arrived. She hesitated as she watched the red light blink on and off. A rush of anticipation, excitement and sheer terror swept over her. She had to do it right. She had to show Blake that she was every bit as good as he was. Calmer, Justine picked up the receiver. "Hello."

The caller was a man with a smooth and even voice. "Ms. Justine Price, please."

"Speaking."

"Ms. Price, I am calling on behalf of Mr. Preston Montgomery, with regard to the temporary position he has open on his personal staff. He would like to know if you could come to Wilson Falls, for an interview this weekend."

"Yes, I think that would be possible."

"Fine, Ms. Price. I have already taken the liberty of arranging a flight and ticket for you. Your ticket is waiting at the charter flight counter, in your name, at Dulles airport. The plane leaves tomorrow morning at 9 and will be landing at Mr. Montgomery's private field. A car will be there to pick you up and bring you to your interview. Is the time acceptable?"

"Yes, that will be fine."

"Have a good flight, Ms. Price."

The caller terminated the call and Justine put the receiver back gingerly. She was feeling particularly pleased with herself. Her "cat got the mouse" smile vanished, as she looked up to find Blake standing in the doorway. He'd been alerted and monitored the call. They hadn't spoken much, since his eruption and subsequent apology. Things had been tense. "Don't do too much smiling yet, Ms. Edwards. We've only got our foot in the door. He hasn't hired you yet, so don't get over confident. We have a long way to go."

Blake certainly knew how to put a damper on a person's spirits. "Nice of him to arrange your transportation. Do you have someone to drive you to the airport?"

"Yes."

"Good. I've already set up my appointments in the Wilson Falls area. I'll be driving down, this afternoon. I'll expect to hear something from you by Saturday evening." Blake turned to leave, then turned back. "Have a good flight."

Justine listened as Blake's footsteps carried him slowly down the hall.

Justine told Steve she was going out of town on business, nothing more. He drove her to the airport and stayed till the plane was high into the air. Steve hadn't told Justine about the job he was interviewing for today... and would most likely get. He'd surprise her, when she got back.

The panoramic view of the Virginia countryside in spring was something poets wrote about and artists painted. The patchwork of fields freshly plowed, and the pastures dotted with horses and cattle, reminded Justine of the calico quilt her mother had made during one long Pennsylvania winter when Justine was a small child. She smiled, thinking back on long forgotten memories of a happy and full childhood.

Justine spent the short flight lost in dreams of her childhood. The plane touched down at a small airstrip far out in the countryside. A red sports car waited on the strip. As the plane turned at the end of the runway, a tall, slim man in his early 20's, with wavy dark hair, walked toward the plane. The gangway was lowered and Justine stepped off the plane with her overnight bag. The tall man moved forward and offered his arm. His eyes betrayed his surprise at seeing her.

"Ms. Price, I'm Armon Dupree. I'm here to take you to your interview with Mr. Montgomery."

Justine recognized the man's voice as the one on the phone. The man escorted her to the car and helped her in, placing her bag behind the seat. He walked back round the car and sat behind the wheel. Before starting the engine he hesitated. Justine detected a small sigh escaping his lips. She wondered what it meant. "I trust you had no problems on your flight, Ms Price?"

"No. The flight was very pleasant."

"Forgive me for being blunt, but you look much younger than the age on your application."

"Thank you, but my age is as I stated. It's genetic. All my family looked younger than they were."

"That's right. You have no relatives... neither do I." There was hurt in the young man's eyes. "Your application was most impressive... and all your references spoke highly of you. How does it come to be that you are out of a job?"

"I wanted to take some time off. Then I decided to look for a more interesting position." The man was suspicious. Justine could read it, not only in his questions, but in his face, as well.

The long ride took them down many picturesque, winding country roads. They passed the occasional car or truck in what seemed a surge of speed. In reality, they were moving at only 45 mph. Armon watched Justine clinch the seat as they passed a slow moving pickup truck. "I'm not driving that fast. You can relax, I know these roads quite well. The people who live around here are never in much of a hurry. They tend to clutter up the road."

Armon had slipped a hint of his feeling of superiority. Justine examined his few words and phrases, during the drive, in an attempt to build a mental record of this man's psyche. Knowing how an adversary thought and felt could be an invaluable weapon if it came down to a battle.

Justine was not prepared for the splendor that met her eyes, as they passed through the pillared gates. Intricately detailed gardens, with fountains, interrupted the manicured lawns here and there. Walkways and arches and benches depicted both modern and classical influences. Tall sculptured hedges loomed up on the right as the house, more like a palace, popped into view. At least a part of the house must have been 18th century. It had been adeptly reworked, adding many more sections to the original house. Justine expected there would be a pool, a tennis court, probably a gym, and all the other luxuries that might spring to mind.

Armon stopped the car, then came round and opened Justine's door. Swiftly, he snatched her bag from the back and showed her to the door. With a confident air he rang the bell and they waited. Justine could hear a woman's footsteps moving, quickly, toward the door. A woman dressed in grey and white answered. She seemed startled. "Uh... Come in Mr. Dupree. Mr. Montgomery will meet you and... Ms. Price on the patio. Lunch will be served in 20 minutes. There is coffee on the patio." The woman's speech was rapid and flustered.

Armon all but pushed Justine through the door. "Thank you Mrs. Gibson. That will be all."

Armon placed Justine's bag on the floor, near the wall. "If you'll follow me, Ms. Price..."

Justine followed Armon through a large, overfurnished room, onto the patio beside the pool. Armon helped himself to coffee and asked Justine if she'd like some. Justine declined. She was already uptight; adding caffeine certainly wouldn't help. Instead, she walked to the poolside and watched the ripples on the pool as the spring breeze moved over it's surface. It was getting warmer now, especially here on the patio, with the sun peeking through the newly leaved trees.

Back in the entry hall, someone picked up Justine's bag and placed it on the entry table. The bag was opened and the contents, as well as the bag, examined thoroughly. Particular interest was given to the feminine undergarments. The bag was closed and replaced, in its previous position near the wall.

Justine continued to stare into the water, until she heard someone speak her name. She turned to find the infamous Preston Montgomery, only a few feet from her. He was a formidable man... tall, muscular, with styled blonde hair, impeccably dressed... and more handsome than his pictures had portrayed. "Ms. Price..." Montgomery offered his hand, "... I'm Preston Montgomery. Won't you sit down?"

Montgomery indicated she sit in one of the chairs at the table. Justine sat and Montgomery sat across from her. Armon remained in the background. "So Ms. Price, do you think you might like working out here in the country? It's quite different from the city."

"I'm originally from Pennsylvania farm country, Mr. Montgomery. I enjoy country life."

"There would also be a substantial amount of travel. Do you have a problem with that?"

"No, no problem."

Mr. Montgomery leaned back in his chair and took a long hard look at Justine. Skillfully, Justine held his eyes on hers.

Mrs. Gibson interrupted to serve lunch. "We'll eat lunch Ms. Price, then we'll talk some more. Join us Armon."

Lunch consisted of a cold seafood platter, tomato juice, French bread, and white wine. Justine only sipped the wine, to be social. The food was expertly prepared, but Justine was too tense to fully appreciate it. In between bites, Montgomery managed to play 20 questions, but the number was closer to 40.

They relaxed a few moments at the finish of the meal, then Montgomery stood. "Armon, I believe you have some things to attend to. Ms. Price and I will be taking a walk through the gardens."

Montgomery offered Justine his arm. She took it and they walked down from the patio along a slate walkway, lined with shrubs and spring flowers. Montgomery continued to bombard her with questions, under the guise of pleasant conversation. Justine caught him asking the same questions in different form, and confronted him about it.

"Mr. Montgomery, I believe I have answered all your questions. I'm sure you've scrutinized my application and investigated me. If you still aren't satisfied, I don't know what else I can say. I believe my work record and my references should speak for me. I would enjoy the challenge I think would come from working for you. But, yours is not the only offer I have at the moment. At this point, I feel the decision rests with you. If you don't mind, I'd like to make a call to arrange for a hotel for the night. I've already checked with the airport and I can't get a flight back until tomorrow."

Mr. Montgomery made no response.

"May I use your phone?" Justine managed to appear only slightly annoyed.

"Ms. Price... if I wanted you to start tomorrow, could you arrange it... on such short notice?"

Justine took a moment to examine Mr. Montgomery's face. "It is rather short notice."

"Yes, I realize that, but could you arrange it?"

Justine took another moment, before she answered. "Yes. I believe it would be possible."

"Then, you're hired. No need for a hotel. You have a choice. There are 15 empty rooms in the house or you may have the East Cottage."

"I think the cottage. Could I see it?"

"Of course. Let's go back to the house and I'll have Mrs. Gibson show it to you."

The cottage was only a short walk from the main house. It nestled shyly amongst a group of ancient cedars. It was not large, but it was comfortably furnished and brightly decorated. Justine felt it would be better, if she could keep this distance between Montgomery and herself. "This is lovely, Mrs. Gibson."

Mrs. Gibson didn't answer. She just stared at the bed.

"Mrs. Gibson... is something wrong?"

Mrs. Gibson seemed startled by Justine's question. "Oh... no ma'am... nothing."

Justine knew the woman was lying, but didn't press her for an answer. "I need to use the phone to arrange for my things to be sent to me."

"Certainly, ma'am. There is no phone here. If you'll follow me back to the house, I'll show you to a phone."

The phone Mrs. Gibson indicated for her use was in the library. One entire wall of the library was covered with bookshelves. It looked like an investment library, as opposed to a library for enjoyment. Many of the books were old, though in good condition. A large tapestry hung from another wall, depicting a scene from some mythical land of unicorns and fairies. Justine wondered which of Montgomery's elicit activities had netted him the wealth of this room.

The windowed French doors in the library overlooked the front gardens and opened onto a slate terrace. Justine used her credit card to place the long distance call to her fictitious number in Washington. She spoke as if the person on the other end were a friend and the agent at the other end did the same. "Hi, Melanie. I got the job. But I have to start tomorrow. I can buy a few things here to hold me, until you send my things. Here's the address..." Justine gave "Melanie" the address and told her she'd call in a few days to let her know how things were going.

Mr. Montgomery had entered the room, during the conversation and waited for Justine to hang up the phone. "Ms. Price, Armon will drive you into town and you may pick up whatever you think you'll need, till your own things arrive. Charge them to me. Armon will take care of it. Stop in at The Fashion Place and have them fit you for something appropriate for a formal dinner party. There will be one here on Tuesday. Do you ride Ms. Price?"

"Yes."

"Then please, pick up some informal clothing... jeans, shirts, whatever." Montgomery seemed distracted.

"Thank you."

"Yes... well. I will be away the rest of the day and part of tomorrow. If you need anything, Armon will see to it. He is waiting for you outside."

Justine collected her purse and started toward the front door. "By the way, Ms. Price... welcome aboard."

"Thank you, Mr. Montgomery." Justine smiled politely, trying not to show her pleasure in too great an amount.

Armon chauffeured Justine about the town, on all her errands. He was not as full of questions as he had been previously. He did, however, instruct the woman at The Fashion Place in what, he felt was appropriate for the dinner. Justine took no exception with his choices as, in this case, he probably knew best. Justine was feeling a bit like a child loose in a toy store. This was the second time she'd been given carte blanche on a shopping spree. What they weren't taking with them, Armon instructed be sent to the estate. Armon stuffed the packages into the car. "We'll go back to the estate, you can freshen up and change. The staff is off this evening, so we'll go out for dinner... say around 7."

Armon was adept at giving instructions and making decisions. Justine had no doubt that Armon wheeled a volume of power in the Montgomery empire. They drove back to the estate at a slow pace, as Armon ran her on a tour of the surrounding countryside. He pointed out several historical interests and some of the larger estates. The area appeared to be a hot bed of "new money"... Country gentlemen and women around every curve.

Armon dropped Justine and her treasures at the cottage, and went on to the main house. Justine showered and changed, into a moderately dressy outfit... somewhere between business and an evening out. Armon was back to pick her up promptly at 7. They drove far out into the woods, to what looked like an English inn. There were many expensive cars parked outside. The maitre d' recognized Armon immediately, and signaled a waiter. "Take Mr. Dupree to Mr. Montgomery's table."

The interior reflected an elegant era of English history. A large stone fireplace stood in the middle of the room, glassed in on two sides. The firelight flickered and danced on the deeply polished wood floors, making them seem almost fluid. Though the lights were dim, Justine saw a room full of beautiful, well dressed people. She felt their eyes on her, as she and Armon skirted past their tables, toward the one single table on the upper level near the large windows. It was without doubt, the best table in the house. They were seated and the waiter left the menus. Justine tried for some information. "Armon, why is everyone looking at me?"

"Don't worry about it. They've just never seen you before. Eventually, nearly every one of them will be up here to say hello and ask about Mr. Montgomery. They'll be trying to find out who you are. Don't converse with them. I'll answer their questions. Now, what would you like to eat? The Beef Wellington is quite good."

"That's fine."

"Would you like wine?"

"No, thank you." Armon was polite, knowing all the right things to do and say, but he was distant and mechanical. Justine tried to probe his interior, but was immediately locked out.

Just as Armon had said, as the meal progressed, the rich and the richer visited the table, fishing for information. Armon was polite but curt, forcing each visitor away from the table, in an unspoken manner. Justine was surprised by the appearance of Blake at the door, with a wealthy young woman on his arm. The woman had, obviously, been there before. Justine wondered how Blake had arranged this. Before being seated at their table, the woman spotted Armon and all but dragged Blake with her, to Armon's table. Armon noticed her traveling toward them and groaned.

"Great."

"What?"

"Nothing."

"Armon... where have you been? Why I haven't seen you or Mr. Montgomery for months. And who is this Armon? One of your new conquests?"

"Ms. Cavanaugh, Mr., Montgomery does not like me to discuss his business. You know that."

"Ah, so she's Mr. Montgomery's business." Ms. Cavanaugh turned catty. "One of his new talent discoveries no doubt."

"Ms. Cavanaugh, if you will excuse us, we would like to finish our meal."

"Of course." The woman tossed back her head, giving the appearance of a huff. Wrapping her arm tightly, around Blake's, she went back to her own table.

"That woman is the biggest busybody this side of the mountain. You notice no one else was so bold as to ask who you were? That gives you an idea of how dangerous she can be. The wrong word and it would be all over the valley by daybreak. Don't let her work on you for information."

"I won't."

Justine made another attempt to pry information from Armon. "What exactly do you do for Mr. Montgomery?"

"Whatever needs to be done."

"I see." The stone wall knocked her down, again.

"You won't be with Mr. Montgomery all that long, this position is only temporary. So, I would suggest you stick to your job and don't try to figure out anyone else's."

"I'm sorry I said anything. I was just trying to understand so I could do my job as well as possible."

Armon's expression softened, ever so slightly. "No, I'm sorry. I'm just so used to people trying to pump me for information, I get a little touchy." He still wasn't going to tell her anything.

As Justine was finishing her desert, she noticed Blake leaving his table and heading back toward the restrooms. She waited until he was out of sight, then excused herself to the ladies' room. Once in the hallway outside the rest room, she feigned dropping her purse and spilling the contents, as an excuse to converse with Blake.

Blake didn't make eye contact with her. "Everything OK?"

"So far."

"I'm a guest at Ms. Cavanaugh's. She knows most of what goes on in Wilson Falls. You can reach me there in an emergency."

Blake went back to Ms. Cavanaugh. It was obvious he was charming the pants off of her. Justine wished she knew if that were literally or figuratively. She gave her face a light dusting, then returned to Armon.

Armon stood, as she approached the table. "Shall we go?" Justine nodded, yes, and they left the restaurant.

Ms. Cavanaugh turned dagger filled eyes on them, till they were through the door.

They drove quietly, back to the estate. Armon stopped the car just inside the gate, got out, and walked back to the gate. Using the same card he'd used to open the gate, he opened an electrical panel and flipped some switches. The gates closed, locked, and a sizzling sound, like electrical current bridging, began. Armon drove to the main house, stopping at the front door. "Come inside. I have to restart all the night security. Then I'll introduce you to the dogs."

"Dogs?"

"Guard dogs. If they don't know you, you won't be able to go outside, once they are loose." Armon went into the library, opened another panel, behind the tapestry, and threw more switches, then relocked the box.

"I guess I should either feel very safe... or be very afraid."

"What do you mean?"

"With all this security, it would seem there is some kind of danger."

"Nothing for you to worry about. Mr. Montgomery is a wealthy man. The security is to keep out would be thieves... and unwanted guests. If you'll follow me we'll go to the kennel."

Justine followed Armon to the back of the house, where the kennels were located. There in the runs, were six large Rottweilers. They barked furiously as the two approached. "Do you always wear the same perfume?"

"Yes."

"Good. Don't change it, while you're here."

Armon opened the first gate. He spoke to the dog and brought him to Justine. Justine was not afraid of dogs, so she was not afraid when Armon asked that she allow the dog to smell her hand. The dogs were highly trained and responded instantly to Armon's commands. He followed this same procedure with each dog until all six were loose on the grounds.

"It will take a few days for them to get fully aware of you, so don't go running around in the dark, without myself or one of the staff." Armon walked Justine back to the cottage, said good night, and went back to the main house.

Justine lay in bed, too tired to sleep. She was proud of herself for handling everything so well and landing the position. Blake couldn't say she wasn't doing a good job... so far. Her smile stayed in place, even after she fell asleep.

Chapter 4

The travel alarm began to buzz at 7:30. Lazily, Justine switched it off and lay in bed, wondering why she'd set the alarm so early... it being Sunday. The dogs were barking wildly in the distance. Justine slipped on her robe and walked to the window, in time to see Armon running across the lawn toward the sounds of the dogs. As he moved out of sight, Justine donned jeans and T-shirt and stole out of the cottage after him. By the time she was within sighting distance, it appeared whatever the dogs had been after, had gone back over the wall.

Justine watched a moment, then started back to the house. She heard Armon dismiss the dogs. Then, she heard the sounds that told her they'd picked up her scent. She knew she couldn't outrun them. Up ahead was a tree, with a large bough she could reach. With a burst of energy, she leapt upward, wrapping her hands over the limb, and pulled herself up into the tree. She'd have to think fast now. The dogs pranced and paced below the tree as they barked. Armon approached, gun drawn, looking mean. He laughed out loud in spite of himself, at the sight of her standing in the tree.

33

He put his gun away and stood just below Justine, looking up. "Would you like to tell me what you're doing?"

"I was taking a walk. I figured they would be locked up by now."

"It's Sunday. Nobody gets up this early."

"You're up."

Armon smiled at her, dismissed the dogs, and helped her down from the tree. Despite her attire being most casual and thrown on, Justine's basic sexuality was still strongly evident. She did the same for jeans and a shirt as she did for suits and gowns. Her body boldly flaunted the fact that she was all woman. Armon was not unaware of Justine's effect. He found himself holding her close, long after her feet touched the ground. "You know... you're awfully attractive."

"Thank you."

Armon started to kiss Justine, but she pushed him away. "I never mix business with pleasure."

"Ha! You're going to have a hell of a time trying to keep them straight on this job. With Mr. Montgomery and his associates, it gets pretty well mixed up."

"I'll do my best to keep things straight."

Armon cracked a knowing little smile. "I bet you will. Come to the house with me. Mrs. Gibson doesn't start work today till 1. I'll make us an omelet."

"Good looking, and he cooks, too?" Justine chided Armon.

Armon took the chide in good humor. "OK... we're even. You want breakfast or not?"

"Indeed I do. Lead on."

During breakfast Justine tried, again, to loosen Armon's tongue. He still wasn't talking. After the meal, Armon collected the empty plates and dropped them in the sink. "So, Ms. Price, what will it be? A swim. A ride, tennis... a movie?"

"I'm not feeling particularly athletic yet this morning. How about a movie?" Justine wanted a chance to explore more of the house... and that couldn't be done from the pool, tennis court, or stable.

"Follow me."

Armon led Justine to the lower level of the house. As they entered the viewing room, Justine made note that the room was sound proofed, with no windows, and only the one door. A perfect place for a murder or assault. This thought uneased Justine. There were rows and rows of video cassettes on the shelves. The seating was informal and comfort conscious. "Have a seat." Armon motioned toward the couch. "Do you have a preference?"

"No. You pick."

Armon turned on the VCR and popped in the tape. As the titles moved over the large screen, Armon switched off the lights and sat at the opposite end of the couch. Justine was instantly aware that she should have chosen the film. She had failed to remember Mr. Montgomery's intense interest and involvement in pornography. Quickly, she analyzed her situation and realized Armon was testing her, looking for a reaction. Justine decided the best course was to take an analytical view toward the film and set aside its content, critiquing the film for form and story line. She could feel Armon watching her. With the eye of a critic, Justine remained cool and detached even at seeing things she never imagined possible. Luckily, the film was only 40 minutes long. Armon left the couch, switched on the lights and ejected the tape. He turned a smirky smile on Justine. "What did you think?"

"Well... the plot was a little thin. The acting was only fair. As just a flat piece of pornography, I guess it's par, but it certainly isn't quality work."

Armon looked surprised. "You have a good eye. It is just a piece of trash, but it was cheap to make and the profits are out of sight, on this stuff. I'm glad to see you aren't a prude. The dinner party on Tuesday is for some of Mr. Montgomery's associates in the 'business'. You are going to have your hands full dealing with that multi-lingual bunch."

"Multi-lingual? I only speak French and German."

"No. No. It's a joke... Roman hands and Russian fingers." Armon smiled and shook his head.

"Oh." Justine was mildly embarrassed at missing the meaning. "How does Mr. Montgomery's regular assistant deal with them?"

"Mr. Montgomery's regular assistant is a man."

"Oh."

"So, you want to see a real movie now, or do something else?"

"I think some fresh air would be nice."

"A ride?"

"Yes."

Armon looked at his watch. "Pat is at the stable by now. Tell him what kind of mount you want. He'll fix you up."

"What about you?"

"I have some work to do. Can you find your way out?"

"I think so."

Justine was relieved to close the door on Armon and the room. Once outside, the scary feeling in the pit of her stomach was banished by the warming spring sun. Without haste, Justine made her way to the stable. She found a man there, busily grooming a horse, with his back to her. "Excuse me. Armon said you could fix me up with a mount."

The man turned to face her and was, for a moment, speechless, looking as if he'd seen a ghost.

"You are Pat aren't you?"

"Uhh... yeah... yeah, I'm Pat."

"Could you fix me up with a nice ride? Something not too spirited."

"Yeah... sure." He was still staring, as if in a trance.

"Is something wrong?"

"Uhh... no, no. I'll get you a horse, right away."

The man literally stumbled away. This had been the third person to show outward signs of surprise at seeing her. What did they know? Pat saddled a horse and led it out of the stable. Justine mounted, noting that Pat had recently imbibed in liquid spirits. What was it about seeing her that drove him, so quickly, to the bottle? Justine rode away slowly toward the trails, all the time aware that Pat was still watching.

As the morning wore on, Justine wound her way through the wooded trails. She was suddenly aware that she was not alone. There was another presence in the woods. Cautiously, she stopped the horse and listened. There was a rustling in the trees just ahead. The pace of her heartbeat quickened, as all her senses leapt to attention. Relief flooded her body, as Blake's face appeared from between the branches.

"You alone?" He whispered.

"Yes."

Blake left the bushes and stood near the horse. "So what have you got so far?"

"Not much, Mr. Montgomery won't be back till this afternoon sometime. Armon has been testing me. There is going to be a dinner party here, on Tuesday night. You might be able to wrangle an invitation through one of his pornography contacts. That's what the dinner is for."

"Getting an invitation has got to be easier than getting in here any other way. I nearly lost the seat of my pants to those dogs, this morning." Justine tried not to chuckle.

"This place is tighter than Fort Knox. We received confirmation that the shipment has not yet been made. See what you can find about a delivery coming in, from North Carolina."

"I'll see what I can do. I expect he'll show me around the office tomorrow."

Blake watched Justine's face as she spoke. His expression changed, slightly. "Are you alright?"

Maybe he was just concerned for her, but Justine took offense. "I am capable of doing my job, Mr. Hampton. If there's nothing else, I better be getting back."

"No... nothing."

Justine jerked back on the reigns, turned the horse and galloped back down the trail. Blake stood on the trail until she disappeared from view.

Justine rode the horse hard, back to the stables. Both she and the horse were winded when they arrived. She handed the horse over to Pat, who was well under the influence of the bottle. "Thank you, Pat."

"Anytime... Ms. Nora."

Even as drunk as he was, Pat knew he'd made an error. From the whiteness of his face... a grave error, in his mind. He moved away, before Justine could pursue his statement. Not wanting to cause waves, Justine started back to the cottage. Armon called to her, as she passed the pool. "Ms. Price..."

Justine stopped to listen. "Yes?"

"Will you be joining me for lunch?"

"Yes. I'm going to shower and change, then I'll be back." Armon waved he understood and Justine continued to the cottage.

By the time Justine returned to the main house, the aromas of lunch in preparation were streaming from the kitchen.

Justine entered from the patio by the pool, into the large overfurnished room. Finding herself alone, she seized the opportunity to examine the room at length.

She checked through drawers, looked for a safe, secret panels, any hiding place that might afford a shred of information. The room was a blank. It had nothing to offer for her efforts. The library was her next project.

The library also bore no fruit for her labors. Disappointed, Justine stepped back into the hall. There was a storage room beneath the stairs, and a small bedroom near the kitchen. Both were clean and neat, almost too neat. Everything was too neat, no magazines lying around, no newspapers, note pads, nothing. It became clearer to Justine how Montgomery had eluded the Bureau for so long. He was meticulously careful.

Justine followed the smell of the food into the kitchen. Mrs. Gibson was busy at her preparations. She was startled, when she turned and saw Justine in the doorway. The plate she was carrying slipped from her hands, and smashed upon the floor. Justine hurried to help Mrs. Gibson.

"I'm sorry. I didn't mean to frighten you." Mrs. Gibson's eyes were glued on Justine's face. "What is it Mrs. Gibson? Why does everyone keep staring at me?"

A voice boomed from behind Justine. "Ms. Price. Leave Mrs. Gibson to her work please." Mr. Montgomery's voice was stern and his face equally unyielding.

"Yes Mr. Montgomery." Justine followed Mr. Montgomery's direction to leave the room.

"Please wait for me in the library."

"Yes, Mr. Montgomery." As Justine moved down the hall toward the library, she could hear Mr. Montgomery talking in low tones to Mrs. Gibson, though she could not hear the words.

Nervously, but trying not to show it, Justine stood at the French doors, looking out, waiting. Had she blown it?

The stern look still covered Montgomery's face as he entered the library and stood before Justine. But, as he spoke, moment by moment, his expression softened and changed. The more he looked into Justine's face, the more yielding he became until finally, he was smiling at her. He had made it clear that Justine was not to interfere with any of the staff and was to pay strict attention to her own duties. Justine indicated she understood and stated Mrs. Gibson's accident had been her fault. She took full responsibility and wished Mr. Montgomery not be cross with Mrs.Gibson. Justine had effectively disarmed her adversary. She had managed to control the situation and come out on top. She was feeling pleased with herself. She was going to nail this perverse creature now standing before her. She was the proverbial wolf in sheep's clothing. She would wait and watch and catch him off guard. The hunter was now the hunted.

Lunch was a success, Montgomery was totally at ease with Justine, as if he'd known her a long time. Armon seemed distracted during the meal. It was almost as if he were annoyed with Montgomery for taking Justine's attention away from him. "If you will excuse us, Ms. Price, Armon and I have a few things to go over. If you don't mind working today, I would like to go over my schedule with you after dinner. Dinner will be at 7. Feel free to do whatever you please until then."

Justine nodded.

"By the way, we don't dress for dinner unless we have guests. When it's just us, wear what you like."

Armon and Montgomery left the table and went into the library. Justine waited till the library door closed, then followed them.

She moved steadily down the hall and stood outside the door trying to hear the conversation. Montgomery was speaking to Armon in an anxious tone. "Did you do as I asked?"

"Yes. I checked her out."

"And?"

"And... she doesn't mix business with pleasure."

"What about the film. How did she react?"

"Very matter of fact. She saw the film for what it was... a low budget piece of pornography, with less than proficient acting. She was neither offended nor put out. But, at the same time, she didn't get into it either. She's not a 'prim and proper fanatic', but she's not trampy either. The lady's got class... Remind you of anyone?"

There was a pause and movement, before Montgomery spoke. "Yes... very much."

Mrs. Gibson was coming down the hall. Justine dashed through the overfurnished room and out across the patio.

Thoughtfully, Justine made her way back to the cottage. Over and over, in her mind, she kept wondering who it was everyone saw when they looked at her. She plunked herself down in the big chair on the cottage porch. She was impatient to get on with her assignment, but knew she mustn't push. She must follow Montgomery's lead and take it slow and easy. This was too important; to her personally, as well as the Bureau, to spook the quarry. She must stalk him, unseen, unfelt and unheard, until she was in striking position.

With a pensive smile, Justine thought back on the trip to Africa she'd taken with her parents, shortly before their deaths. The photographic safari into the bush country was full of excitement, fear and terror. She had imagined herself as the lioness... controlled and powerful. She'd always had the feeling she'd been a cat of prey in another life. She enjoyed feelings of power and running on the edge. Walking the fence with tigers on the left and crocodiles on the right, as it were. Her decision to change careers had come following that trip. This assignment would be the test of her ability to survive and surmount, in an uncertain country with uncertain terrain and predators around every turn. Any moment might find her tripping into a pit of "vipers" or being beset by "lions". One thing she learned in the jungle: seeming tranquility must not be taken at face value. Behind it lurked unknown horrors... maybe even death. The drums of Africa echoed through her mind as she sat, eyes closed, clutching the pillow from the chair. Slowly, she leaned back her head and felt the rush of anticipation, the ripple of electricity that traveled through her body. The experience was sensuous, almost sexual. The thrill of the unknown, the walk on the wild side of herself... The self no one knew.

Armon stood at a distance, watching Justine languishing in the warmth of her memories. After several long moments he swallowed hard, his face moved to emotion by something from his own memory, then walked away. Justine never knew he'd been watching. The noisy chatter of a squirrel high in the trees beyond the ancient cedars, drew Justine from the past to the present. She smiled to herself at hearing the squirrel's excessive chatter, then left the porch and stole toward the sound. Though she was still a good 20 feet away, the squirrel became frightened and scurried away, branch to branch, then out of sight.

A glint of something shiny twinkled up at Justine, from the leaf-covered ground, just ahead. Carefully, she uncovered the object and found it to be a silver hair comb, in the shape of a feather. A flicker of recognition darted through her mind. She had seen one like it before, but where? Her mouth moved to a pout and her brow tightened, as she became annoyed with herself for not having full recollection. Delicately, she fingered the comb as if to coax the answers from it. But, still, her mind could not form a picture. Tossing the comb from one hand to the other, she walked back to the cottage and inside. She flopped across the bed, studying the small adornment in her hands. Then, rolled to her back, holding the comb at arm's length above her. There was no doubt in her mind that she had seen the twin to this piece... but where? In an attempt to clear her mind, Justine closed her eyes. The excitement and stress of her current situation had robbed her of much energy. Once her eyes closed, her body warmly welcomed the opportunity for rest and she was asleep.

Justine's eyes popped open, as the knock upon the door roused her from the stillness of her sleep. The deep shadows in the room told her the day was fading. Not yet fully awake, she found her way to the door. Armon stood... young and handsome... before her, but his face wore the lines of concern. "Are you alright, Ms. Price?"

"Yes. I must have fallen asleep."

"Mr. Montgomery is waiting dinner for you."

"I'm sorry. Let me change and I'll be right along."

"I'll wait for you."

Armon waited on the porch. Hastily, Justine changed and joined him. She was surprised at the leisurely pace by which Armon was traveling. Weren't they late? Wasn't Mr. Montgomery waiting? Armon led the way into the dining room. Mr. Montgomery was seated at the head of the table. He rose as Justine entered.

"I apologize for being late. I hadn't meant to fall asleep."

"No matter. Please." Montgomery held the chair at his left for Justine.

Dinner was more than adequate and much more than Justine could eat. "You haven't touched your wine Ms. Price. Is it not to your liking? I could have something else brought up."

"Oh, no. I'm sure it's fine. But, you said you wanted to do some work after dinner. I want to be sure my head is clear."

"Very wise, Ms. Price. Armon, if you are finished, please see to the security. Ms. Price and I will be in my office."

Finally, she was going to see the office. Now things were progressing. Montgomery helped Justine from her chair, took her arm, and ushered her up the stairs, into the west wing.

There was no doubt that Mr. Montgomery was excessively wealthy. All the furnishings and art work in the rooms they passed, were strictly top drawer. They stopped at the end of the hall, in front of two massive mahogany doors. "These doors were imported. Cost me a small fortune, but they are worth it. They are magnificent aren't they?"

"Yes. Very impressive."

Justine was not impressed. She was anxious. Anxious to get inside. Montgomery opened the doors, onto a large elegant office. The drapes were drawn, but the light on the desk threw enough light to display the room. Montgomery walked to a door on the left, and opened it onto a smaller office... not as fancy, but a cut above most offices.

"This is where you will work, Ms. Price. I think you'll find everything you need... somewhere in here. If not, Armon knows where everything is. Now, if you'll get the appointment schedule, from the desk, and bring it out, I'll update my schedules with you."

Justine went to the desk, picked up the leather bound appointment book and returned to the outer office. Mr. Montgomery had already seated himself behind the ornate antique desk. He motioned for Justine to sit, in the chair beside his desk. Reluctantly, she did so. The chair placed her closer to Montgomery than she felt, was a proper distance. But she wasn't going to rock the boat. They went over plans and schedules. The dinner party Tuesday, seemed to be Montgomery's particular interest. It would be an important business, as well as pleasure, function. The one thing on the schedule that caught Justine's attention was a flight scheduled for Rockham, North Carolina. This could be the connection. She'd pass this on to Blake, as soon as possible. "Oh, Ms. Price, I think I'd like you to fly down with me... to Rockham."

"Yes, sir."

Justine couldn't have asked for a better setup. She could find out first hand, what the trip to Rockham would develop. Wouldn't Blake be impressed. Maybe not. Maybe he was jealous of her getting the assignment. But why? He was well ahead of her in the Bureau. She couldn't possibly pose a threat to him.

Sometimes it was hard to figure why people would be jealous or envious of another person's achievements. Maybe Blake was insecure, although he certainly never let it show. Justine's mind wandered in the moments Montgomery had not spoken. When he picked up again, Justine was lost. But she regained her senses, without his noticing.

They covered all activities through the end of the next month. "Paul Carver, the man you are filling in for, should be back the end of next month. I must say though, I won't be glad to see you leave. You are much nicer to look at than he is."

Justine lowered her eyes and smiled shyly.

"Oh, come now Ms. Price. I'm sure you are often complimented. Have you ever considered a career in modeling or acting?"

Justine laughed. This sounded like dialogue from one of his blue movies. "No."

"Don't laugh. I bet you are very photogenic... Let me take your picture and we'll find out."

"No. I don't think so."

"One picture, what can it hurt? I have a studio next to the viewing room. It will only take a few minutes. I can develop it tonight and you can see it in the morning."

"Well..." It sounded like he was attempting to lure her into something... but what? Justine was curious.

"... Alright." Logically, Justine told herself she should do it, to keep herself in good with Montgomery. But in the back of her mind, her own ego played some part in her decision.

"Great. Let's go."

They met Armon on the stairs. "Armon, we'll be in the studio to take a picture or two, then you can take Ms. Price back to the cottage."

Armon's expression was one of dissatisfaction, but he responded in assent, "Alright. I'll wait by the pool."

The studio was fully equipped with state of the art camera and movie equipment. There was even a stage and lighting control panels. The only prop on the stage was a large round bed, covered with a fur throw and many pillows of varying size and shape. Montgomery picked up an expensive looking camera from an equipment covered table against the wall. "What do you think?"

"It is... impressive. Do you actually make your movies here?"

"Oh, no. This is only for my personal use. Sometimes my... associates come here to screen potential "new talent" and they use it. They'll probably put it to good use Tuesday evening. Sit on the edge of the bed there, and smile."

Justine sat casually, on the edge of the bed and Montgomery took the picture. Justine started to rise. "No. Wait. Let me take a few more, then I can develop the whole roll. Lean back on your arms. Yes. That's it. Now tilt your head back and to the side. Good."

Montgomery took a few more pictures, then moved toward Justine. "Mess up your hair a little bit."

Justine questioned what it was he wanted. Rather than explain, he placed the camera on the bed and pushed his hands through her hair. Justine was starkly aware of a change in his expression. His muscles tensed and his face went pale. When Montgomery's hands came to rest on her cheeks, she became frightened.

"Nora."

He spoke in such a soft whisper, Justine could barely discern the name, but it was definitely Nora. Nora must be the woman everyone was seeing when they looked at her. The mystery woman. Montgomery remained fixed, standing before Justine, staring down into her face. Finding her voice, Justine asked the question. "Who is Nora?"

The question snapped Montgomery back from his trip in time.

"Nobody. Nobody. I'll finish out the roll and you can go."

Montgomery's mood had changed, drastically. He was less friendly, almost rude. He clicked the shutter one last time and instructed Justine to go.

Justine found Armon sitting beside the pool, in the moonlight. She couldn't help but wonder how he'd become involved with Montgomery. Armon examined her appearance closely, before he spoke. He rose from the chair and stood in front of her. "Mr. Montgomery usually gets what he wants."

That was more of a question than a statement.

"I suggest you be careful. I'll walk you back to the cottage."

Armon turned and walked away. Justine followed. It took several quick steps to catch up with Armon. They walked in silence, then Justine attempted to shake loose his tongue. "Armon..."

"Yes?"

"It is none of my business. I know that. But... how did you come to work for Mr. Montgomery? You don't seem particularly suited to one another."

Armon stopped and glanced sidelong at Justine. He searched her face, looking for a reason for her question. Justine continued. "I mean, you're a young, attractive man and you seem to be sensitive to others. Mr. Montgomery seems... I don't know... I can't explain it. It's just a feeling."

Armon turned back to the cottage and walked, as he spoke. "Mr. Montgomery took me in 5 years ago, when my mother died. I had no other family. He gave me a place to live and a job. I was only 17 and had no money or relatives."

"I'm sorry about your mother. Maybe I'm just reading Mr. Montgomery wrong."

Armon stopped near the cottage porch. Justine stepped up onto it. "Thank you, Armon. Oh, Armon... Who's Nora?"

Armon's eyes widened with alarm. "Who told you about her?"

"No one told me anything. Mr. Montgomery spoke her name to me... and Pat called me Nora. It's as if they thought I was her. Do I look like this Nora person?"

Armon turned away. "Yes. You look very much like her."

"Who is she?"

Armon hesitated. "She was my... mother."

With that said, Armon moved quickly away toward the house.

Justine's brain pulled the few facts together and her intuition did the rest. Armon's mother, Nora, had been young

and attractive, looking very much like Justine. She had died
5 years ago... The woman without a name that had been so
brutally murdered. That's where she'd seen the silver comb.
In that picture of the woman's body. An intense fear welled
up inside her. A fear like none she'd ever known. In a panic,
she rushed inside the cottage, locking the door behind her.
She wanted out of this place, more than she'd ever wanted
anything. She realized she was near panic and talked to herself. "Wait a minute. I'm a trained agent. I'm not supposed
to go out of control. I have to get a grip on myself. I have
a job to do. I'm not in danger... not yet. They don't know
I know anything. They don't know I'm an agent. I'm safe.
I'm safe."

Her heart rate began to slow and her breathing returned
to normal. Spotting the silver comb on the dresser, she
moved toward it and picked it up. She must get it to Blake.
It was evidence. Maybe not enough to prove anything, but
it was a link. A link between Montgomery and the woman
who, now, had a name... Nora Dupree.

Chapter 5

Mr. Montgomery set a hectic pace for Justine the next morning. Setting aside the fact that Justine knew about all his illicit activity, he was a heavy operator in the legitimate business community. His correspondence load was massive. Mr. Montgomery left the house at 2. In his absence, Justine ran a quick check through the file, but found nothing of interest. He must have another location for the material she was after. Justine began to feel overwhelmed when, by 4, she still couldn't see the end of the work.

Mr. Montgomery returned home around 10, to find Justine still busy at her desk. "Ms. Price... Mrs. Gibson says you didn't come down to dinner. I don't expect you to work all night. Things piled up a bit, when Paul left so unexpectedly, but I don't think one more day will matter much. Here," Montgomery handed Justine a large yellow envelope, "I forgot to give these to you this morning. They're the pictures I took. You are photogenic, just as I said. Justine opened the envelope and examined the professional looking photographs. She was surprised at how nice they had turned out. "I like this one."

Montgomery pointed to a full face shot. It was particularly nice.

"You must be a magician with a camera. I've never had any pictures this good."

"They just didn't see you with my eyes."

Justine again felt uncomfortable. It was hard knowing this man, being so pleasant and charming just on the other side of the desk, was a brutal murderer. Justine tucked the pictures back in the envelope.

"I guess I'll go to the cottage now."

"Don't you want something to eat first?"

"No. I'm not very hungry."

"You can finish this up in the morning. I won't be here. The guests should be arriving around 6 tomorrow night, so be ready by 5:30. The dress you were fitted for came today. I had Mrs. Gibson take it to the cottage... Armon picked it out, didn't he?"

"Yes. He did. How did you know?"

"Just a guess. I'm sure you'll look very nice in it. Well, good night. Armon will see you to the cottage. He's in the library."

"Good night."

Armon had kept well away from Justine, since the previous evening. As they walked, Justine apologized for upsetting him. Armon brushed off the incident. He stopped as the cottage came into view. Abruptly, he said good night and headed back to the big house. It was apparent, he was still upset.

Next morning, Justine finished the mound of paperwork and used Mr. Montgomery's absence to inspect the rooms in the west wing. She came up empty and abandoned her search at 3, in order to get ready for the dinner. She showered, coiffured her hair and lacquered her nails. Once dressed, she stood in front of the floor length mirror to check her appearance. The deep purple satin gown clung to every curve of her body... alterations being perfection. The beading reached up from her waist in an attempt to envelop her bosom. Only a scattered few managed to mount the soft curves and travel toward the valley above. Justine found herself hoping Blake would be at the dinner, if for no other reason than to see how attractive and sensual she was. Certain that Blake would find a way to attend, Justine dropped the silver comb into her evening bag. What information she had so far was, in her mind, less than sufficient. Knowing Blake, she was sure he also would feel the information was insufficient. With one last pleased look at herself in the mirror, Justine turned, left the cottage, walked down the path, and entered the big house from the patio.

She found no one downstairs, but could hear the sounds of dishes and people in the kitchen. Upon entering the kitchen, she found an array of catering people busy at work. Mrs. Gibson was overseeing the activity. Justine sought out Mrs. Gibson, even though it appeared Mrs. Gibson was trying not to notice Justine's presence. "Mrs. Gibson."

Mrs. Gibson looked up at Justine, then away. "Yes, ma'am?"

"I want to apologize for the other day. I guess looking at me is like looking at the past, kinda spooky for you."

Mrs. Gibson looked surprised. "You know?"

"About Nora? Yes. She was Armon's mother, she looked very much like me, and she's dead."

Mrs. Gibson's eyes told Justine there was more to it than those simple facts. "Mrs. Gibson, is there something else I should know?"

Mrs. Gibson started to speak, but Armon appeared in the entry way.

"Ms. Price. Please leave Mrs. Gibson to her work. Mr. Montgomery wants to see you in the game room."

Justine followed Armon, as she thought to herself, why is my timing so bad? Mrs. Gibson knew something and, one way or another, Justine was going to find out what it was.

The game room was, without question, just that. It was enormous and contained every imaginable diversion ever invented. Mr. Montgomery stood at the pool table, racking up the balls. "Ms. Price. You look... outrageously good." Montgomery's smile was only half there. "I usually entertain my guests here, before dinner. Armon will bring them down. You stay here with me."

Armon's manner was somber and affected. He left, with reluctance. "Do you play Ms. Price?"

Justine smiled to herself. Did she play? She played, alright. Father had taught her well. She and her brother Steve, clipped many an unsuspecting hot shot. He'd set 'em up and she'd shoot 'em down.

"Yes, I play."

"Grab a cue. We'll play a little eight ball. You break."

Justine broke, then ran the table. Montgomery looked impressed. "Why do I get the impression I'm being hustled?"

Justine looked smug. Montgomery laughed heartily.

They were even up when the first of the guests arrived. Mr. Montgomery greeted them, then introduced Justine.

The two middle aged men viewed Justine with hungry eyes. Mr. Montgomery took notice and addressed the men. "If you don't mind gentlemen, make yourselves at home. The bartender isn't here yet, so help yourselves. Ms. Price and I are in the midst of a competition. But I'm going to win the next two and it will be over."

Montgomery looked over at Justine, with his own smug expression. Justine raised one eyebrow and moved her lips to a pout. In her mind, his expression was a dare. Montgomery racked up the balls. Justine broke and ran the table. Montgomery's manner changed as the 8 ball was sunk. It struck Justine that she'd made a grave error. Mr. Montgomery didn't like to loose... especially not in front of others. Montgomery broke and ran the table, then insisted on a tiebreaker. Justine broke, sunk two balls, then missed. Justine knew she must loose. Montgomery watched her face a moment, before turning to the table. He knew she'd missed on purpose. Justine hoped the butterflies in her stomach, from realizing her mistake, would be put to rest. The room had filled up with guests, but Montgomery had paid no attention. His attention was totally on the game and Justine. Montgomery ran the table, racked, broke, and ran it again. Justine was relieved when everyone clapped and congratulated Montgomery on his win.

Justine slipped through the crowd and out of the room... in need of some air. She found her way down the corridor, up the stairs, through the over furnished room, and out to the pool. She stood staring down at the lights in the pool. She had almost blown it. She knew that.

Armon approached, from behind. He was nearly at her elbow, when he spoke, "He doesn't like to loose."

Justine was startled, lost her balance and nearly fell into the pool. Armon caught her and held her closely in his arms. He looked lovingly into her eyes. "You remind me so much of my mother. And I miss her so much... just hold me for a minute... the way she used to... just hold me."

Armon wrapped his arms around Justine and placed his head on her shoulder. Justine couldn't help feeling sorry for the boy, who had obviously loved his mother so much. She wrapped her arms around him. Armon kept repeating and repeating how much he missed his mother and how sorry he was. Justine might have learned more about what had happened to Nora had Mr. Montgomery not appeared.

He was furious. "Armon!"

Armon let Justine go, his eyes misty with tears. The look he gave Montgomery should have caused Montgomery to fall to the floor dead. Armon turned and walked away from the house. Montgomery came to stand near Justine. His expression soften, as he spoke. "Armon is very troubled. It would be best not to allow something like that to happen again."

"I'm sorry. I almost fell in the pool and it just..."

"It doesn't matter. Please come back inside."

Montgomery offered Justine his arm and they went to the dinning room where the guests were in the process of being seated.

Justine sat on Montgomery's left. Armon's seat remained empty, through dinner. There was an array of beautiful women around the room, but somehow, Justine stood out. She felt eyes on her all through the meal. There were so many people, it took some time, before she sighted Blake. He was escorting an attractive young hopeful. After the meal, everyone moved to the patio. The evening was warm and the night filled with stars. During dinner the band set up on the balcony and had already begun to play. Montgomery kept Justine close at his side. Several times she tried to work away from him, but he wasn't going to allow it. Finally, she excused herself to the powder room. It was the only place she was sure he wouldn't follow her.

Blake had been watching for his opportunity. Now, spying it, he excused himself and pressed, slowly, through the crowd. Justine made sure Blake didn't loose sight of her. She stepped into the dark library, then out through the French doors, onto the slate terrace. Blake was careful not to be seen and joined her. Justine took his arm, pulled him aside, and began talking. "I don't know how much time we have. Here."

She reached into her bag and produced the silver comb. She pressed it into Blake's hand. "I think you'll find this matches the one in the picture of that dead woman in the file."

Blake glanced at it, then tucked it into his pocket.

"The dead woman may be Nora Dupree, Armon's mother. Montgomery has scheduled a flight for Thursday, to Rockham, North Carolina. I will be going with him. The plane is scheduled to land at a private air strip owned by Gordon Industries. I haven't been able to locate any of his 'special' paperwork. I've narrowed it down to the East wing. Maybe while we're gone Thursday, you could get some people into the house to check it out. I'm not sure if Armon is flying with us or not."

"What was that exhibition in the game room? You're supposed to keep a low profile. And that dress..."

"Mr. Montgomery asked me to play... I lost. And Armon picked out the dress."

"Do you think Armon knows Montgomery killed his mother... if that's who the woman was?"

"I don't think so. I don't know just how involved he is in Montgomery's illegal business. He may not be involved at all. I have no evidence, either way."

"How'd you find out the dead woman's name?" Justine sighed. "I must look more like her than we thought. People who work here act as if they see a ghost, when they look at me. Montgomery accidentally called me Nora. I got

Armon to tell me who she was. *He* even thinks I look like her."

Blake walked away, looking strained and thoughtful. "Maybe we should pull you out."

"This close? Are you crazy?"

"I don't want you to get hurt... or worse. This guy is crazy. He'd have to be to do something so brutal. If you really look that much like her and he thinks he sees her, when he looks at you... there's no telling how he might react. Some little thing might set him off and he'd do it all over again... relive it. It's a very real possibility."

"I'll be careful."

"Well, here." Blake handed Justine a small pistol. "I know we had to send you in unarmed, but you don't have to stay that way."

Justine accepted the pistol and dropped it into her bag.

Footsteps entered the library. Blake reacted instantly, grabbing Justine, and pulling her into his arms. He kissed her passionately and long. Justine realized just how much she had been waiting for this moment. The kiss was every bit as stimulating as she had imagined. Armon stood in the doorway, hatred filling his face. He stepped forward and jerked Blake away from Justine. With murder in his eyes, he pushed Blake further away. Afraid for what Armon might do, Justine spoke. "Armon, I'm glad you're here. Please take me back to the pool."

Armon's jaw was tight and his eyes never left Blake.

"Please, Armon."

Armon turned back to Justine, keeping Blake in the corner of his eye. He took Justine's arm with some degree of force and pulled her back into the house. He still said nothing, left her with Montgomery, and disappeared for the rest of the evening.

After several hours of being grabbed, pinched and generally "felt up", the party began to thin out. Many of the guests were staying the night and had already gone to their rooms. Others had left and still others had gone to the viewing room, or the studio. Blake was with the group in the studio. His young hopeful was taking a "screen test". Most of the guests were so drunk or coked up, they had little idea of what they were doing or who they were with. There were sufficient drugs on the premises to arrest Montgomery, but the Bureau wanted more... they wanted the big shipment... Montgomery... and the seller. They wanted Montgomery away for as long as possible. This would be a minor bust in their eyes. Justine was made uneasy by the rowdiness and uninhabited actions of the guests. Mr. Montgomery, however, was in total control. He turned to Justine. "I think we can leave the rest of them to their own devices now. We may find a few of them scattered around the house in the morning."

Montgomery smiled broadly at Justine. "Listen, I'm sorry for getting so intense with you over a simple game of pool. I fear I frightened you into intentionally throwing the game my way."

Justine didn't answer.

"Let's go to the kitchen and get some coffee."

Justine agreed and followed Montgomery. They came across several couples deeply involved, as they passed down the hall. "Don't mind them. They don't even know we're here."

The kitchen was also being put to use. Montgomery handed Justine a cup of coffee and suggested they find someplace less populated.

Justine followed Montgomery up the stairs and into the east wing. She was glad to get into the east wing. Maybe she could find out something. As they passed the doors along the corridor, the sounds of laughter and ecstasy echoed inharmoniously out into the hall.

They stood before a large set of doors, twins to the ones on his office. Montgomery opened them, onto a palatial living area... an apartment of elegant proportion. Montgomery offered Justine a seat in the livingroom. He sat across from her. "So, tell me about yourself, Ms. Price."

Justine smiled at Montgomery. He was going to check her out; again, watch for a mistake.

"Mr. Montgomery. You know everything there is to know about me. Why don't you tell me about yourself?"

Montgomery eyed Justine over the top of his cup. "I'm not very interesting and I don't know everything about you. You don't smoke, you drink very little, you weren't interested in any of the drugs at the party... do you have any vices, Ms. Price?"

"I guess that would depend on what you call a vice."

"Do you have a boyfriend... a lover?"

"I don't see where that question would relate to my work."

"It doesn't. I just want to know Justine... the person... not just Justine the personal assistant. Who, I must say, I am impressed as hell with... so far."

"Thank you."

Justine thought before answering Montgomery's original question. It was a 50/50 split, in her own thoughts, on whether she should answer or not. If she didn't answer, he might get angry or start checking further into her cover. If she did answer, he might use it against her. She chanced an answer. "No. Mr. Montgomery. I do not have a boyfriend."

"A lover, then?"

"No."

"There is something very wrong with that, Ms. Price. You are too young and too attractive to be uninvolved."

"I didn't say I'd never been involved... I'm just not involved... at the moment."

"What type of man do you look for?"

Justine looked away, smiling to herself. "I don't have a particular physical type. But, I like someone I can talk easily with, someone who enjoys life, someone who likes to dance..."

"You like dancing? Why didn't you say something at the party?"

Montgomery rose and moved toward the bar. He flipped a switch and soft music filled the room. "Let's dance." Montgomery held his hand out to Justine.

"Mr. Montgomery..."

"Come on, now. This is my party. Won't you dance with the host?"

Justine decided it best to accept his offer. She took his hand and he began to guide her around the room. By the second song, the lights began to dim. Justine looked up at them. "Power failure?"

Montgomery laughed. "No. They're set on a timer. If it bothers you, I can reset it."

"No, that's alright."

Justine was well aware that Montgomery was trying to seduce her. Her only worry was his reaction when she finally would have to turn him down. Could she effectively handle it without making him angry? If it were any other man, she wouldn't hesitate. If the man got angry it was his problem. However, if it were any other man, she might not have to turn him down. Justine had never given much thought to sleeping with a man for the sole purpose of control. If she were to allow his advances to continue and give herself up to him, her position would be greatly fortified. He was not an unattractive man. She wondered how the men in the department handled these situations. Would they refrain from using sex to install themselves in a cover. Would Blake? Had Blake slept with Ms. Cavanaugh? ...or that cute little number on his arm this evening? Would it be viewed differently if she were to use sex as a manipulative tool? Justine buried these questions under the weighted fact that this man, holding her in his arms so tenderly, was a murderer. He tortured and killed the woman named Nora Dupree... Armon's mother. If she surrendered to him, would she... as Blake had intimated... become Nora in his eyes? Would he finally torture and kill her? Or had Nora refused him... and died because of it? These thoughts, no matter how bizarre, were enough to convince Justine to hold her ground. Her thoughts caused a cold shiver to pass over her body. Montgomery was immediately aware of it. His expression was strange and confused. They stopped dancing and he held her at arms length. "What's wrong?"

"I don't know, I think I'm just tired."

Montgomery saw something in her eyes. "You act as if you are afraid of me? Has someone told you something?"

"No, I..." Justine's brain scurried to cover her emotional slip. "... Mr. Montgomery, to tell you the truth... I find you very attractive, but in order to effectively pursue my duties, I must insist we keep our relationship strictly business... at least until such time as I am no longer employed by you."

She added that last touch, hoping he would set his advances aside, with the hope of pursuing them at a later date. Rather than stopping him with a wall, she tried to slow him with a traffic sign.

Montgomery eyed her sternly, moved away, then walked back to her. He laughed out loud. "Ms. Price... you're fired!"

Justine's face fell. "Fired... but..." She couldn't be fired. She had a job to do. She must find a way to recoup.

Montgomery held her arms. "I can't wait until Paul comes back to sever our business relationship, if it means I have to wait to make love to you."

Justine realized she'd miscalculated. Montgomery pulled her into his arms and kissed her passionately. Justine pushed him away. "Mr. Montgomery, I agreed to take this position until your regular person returns. You agreed to pay me for my services, for that period. If you are not a man of your word, Mr. Montgomery, there would be no point in my attempting any relationship with you... of any kind. I despise people who go back on their word."

"If it's the money... I'll pay you all we agreed upon."

"Mr. Montgomery..." Justine wore her best indignant face. "I am not a prostitute. But I am sure, if you require one, there is one to be found somewhere in this house tonight."

Montgomery was outwardly unhappy with Justine's rejection. He was frustrated and angry. After a moment, his face lost the anger and he spoke. "Alright, Ms. Price. I will not have you think my word is worthless. I'll make every effort to put my feelings on hold. But, I cannot promise this will not come up again before Paul returns. I have never professed myself to be a saint. We are all human beings, with our frailties and shortcomings. If you'll excuse me. I'll be right back and I'll take you to the cottage."

Montgomery left the room, then returned five minutes later, looking more composed. He led the way out and Justine followed.

Once outside the house, Montgomery took Justine's arm. She could feel a strange tenseness, moving through his muscles. Neither of them spoke, until Montgomery said good night at the porch. He turned and moved away.

Justine watched, until Montgomery was out of view, then entered the cottage. She felt for the light switch, sure she had left the lights on, when she went out.

Flipping the switch did nothing. She flipped it, again and again. There were no lights. Without warning, someone grabbed her from behind, placed a hand over her mouth and held her tightly. Her heart pounded so furiously, she barely heard what he whispered in her ear. "Take it easy... It's me... Blake."

She all but collapsed in his arms, with relief. He removed his hand, turned her toward him, then whispered again. "Come with me."

Holding her elbow, Blake skirted Justine into the bath, closing the door behind them. He turned on the water. "Just a precaution. What the hell were you doing? I've been waiting over an hour."

Justine sighed. I thought I was going to get a chance to look around the east wing... but I didn't."

"Don't worry about it... I did. Montgomery has a safe in his apartment. We'll get a look inside, while he's away."

Justine felt awkward, remembering Blake's kiss, from earlier. It certainly had been convincing... even to Justine. "You're doing a good job, Ms. Edwards. I guess I was wrong in thinking you weren't ready."

A crooked smile crept over his lips. "I overreacted about the dress. I'd never seen you dressed like that before. You're a real knock out in it. Lot of the others at the party thought so, too. You could have a real career in films. You know, I..."

Justine could no longer control her impulse to kiss him. Throwing her arms around his neck, her lips merged with his. She could not explain her impulsive reactions, other than

60

an awareness of being stimulated by the excitement of the evening and having many emotions lifted to a conscious level. She had no resistance to fight her impulses and it became clear, Blake didn't want her to fight them. Her impulsive action led to his uninhibited reaction. Passion filled both their bodies with heated desire. Forgetting the reality of their place and time, Blake led Justine back into the bedroom. Adeptly, the purple gown was loosened and dropped to the floor. His body pressed hard against hers, as they fell softly upon the bed. Their ardor may have been iced, had they known they were giving a performance. A performance watched on closed circuit television by Montgomery and Armon.

"She lied to me, Armon. She does have a lover. I want you to find out who he is and how she knows him."

"His name is Blake Parrum... We saw him at the Inn with Ms. Cavanaugh."

"Did she act as if she knew him, then?"

Armon didn't answer. Montgomery became aware of Armon's obsessive attention to the monitor screen. "Armon... she is not your mother. She is not Nora. Did she act as if she knew him... at the Inn?"

"No."

"I want to know everything about him."

Armon's expression was angry... even jealous. "I'll find out."

"I don't want him dead, Armon. And I don't want her to know. Just check him out. I'm going to check her out a bit more, too. She's not Nora, but I'm not sure she is who she claims to be, either."

Justine's eyes shown like onyx, under the scattered beams of moonlight that sifted through the curtains. Blake kissed her face and held her close. Then, abruptly, he let her go and left the bed. Justine rose to one elbow and watched, as Blake dressed. He came back to the bed and sat down, facing Justine. He whispered to her. "Get dressed. I'm taking you out of here."

"What?"

"Get dressed. I'm taking you with me."

"But why?"

"I can't leave you here. You might get hurt."

"Blake, that's part of my job. I know the risks... so do you."

Blake's face wrinkled, with concern. "But..."

"Blake... if it was you in my place and I wanted you out..."

"You're right. It has to be separate. But, I don't have to like it."

A quiet smile turned up the corners of Blake's mouth. He kissed Justine one last time, long and hard. "I have to collect the little starlet and get out of here. I'll get everything set for Thursday. If anything changes, let me know... right away."

Justine nodded.

"You be careful."

Justine smiled, while Blake planted an affectionate kiss on her forehead. Blake left cautiously, locking the door behind him. Justine fell back into the pillows, still smiling, and sighed deeply. Two of her fondest wishes had come true... all within the space of days. A big case and the man she yearned to know. She truly must have a fairy godmother. Her smile faded as she thought on her situation. She hoped she had a guardian angel as well.

Chapter 6

Mrs. Gibson appeared at the cottage door, early the next morning, with a breakfast tray and the news that the trip to North Carolina had been moved up. Justine was to be packed and ready to leave by noon. Justine ate a few bites of breakfast, but she was simply too nervous. Then she packed her things, dressed, and carried her bag to the big house. There appeared to be no one around. Seizing the moment, Justine dropped her bag in the hall and slipped into the library. She dialed the Washington number. Mr. Montgomery appeared just as the call was answered. Justine pretended she hadn't seen him.

"Hello, Melanie. How are you?..That's good. Listen, I realized I hadn't given you a number to reach me. It's 555-2980. Everything is fine. It's all very exciting... As a matter of fact, I'm flying off to North Carolina, in just a few hours... Yeah. I am lucky. Give Bobby my love." That line was coded for "advise control immediately". "Bye, Melanie."

Justine acted surprised at seeing Mr. Montgomery. "Oh, Mr. Montgomery. I hope you don't mind. I forgot to give

Melanie the number when I called for my things."
Montgomery said nothing. "Well, I'm all packed and ready
to roll. Is there anything from the office I should bring?"

Montgomery eyed her a moment. "Just a note pad should
be all you'll need. We may be staying a few days. I'm not
sure exactly when my business contact will arrive. It will
be sometime between now and Saturday."

"Oh, I just packed for today and tomorrow."

"You can buy whatever you need when we arrive.

Justine thought to herself, how wonderful it must be to
feel so free about spending money. She started for the office
to collect a pad. Montgomery followed along behind her. He
stood in the office door, watching her tuck the notepad,
some pencils, and pens, into her bag. "Ms. Price... did you
see anyone you knew at the party last night?"

"No."

Montgomery blocked Justine's exit from the room. "Then
would you mind telling me who the man was coming out
of the cottage early this morning?"

Justine was caught off guard. Immediately, she took a
defensive stance. "Am I being watched, Mr. Montgomery?
Have I no privacy?"

"We try to keep a tight security here, Ms. Price. I have
many things of value on the grounds. I like to know what
goes on here... who comes and who goes. Who was he?"

Justine turned on an embarrassed face. "I don't know his
name."

"What was he doing at the cottage?"

Unsure of just how much of what went on in the cottage
Montgomery was aware of, Justine felt it best not to stray
too far from the truth. Looking straight into Montgomery's
face, with teary eyes, she spoke unevenly, as if not wanting
to tell. "Well... he... I... He made love to me."

Justine appeared to break down, feigning tears. "I don't
know exactly how it happened."

Justine pulled a hanky from her purse and held it to her
face. "I guess I just got caught up with the party and the
atmosphere you set last night. He was there waiting... it...
I..."

Montgomery was thrown off kilter by her frankness and unexpected tears. He hesitated. "His name is Blake Parrum. He's a high-ticket real estate agent for individuals and private industry. I don't know him. He came with one of the new recruits... You don't have to worry about seeing him, again. I've seen to it that he'll be out of town by the time we return."

Justine tried not to show her concern. What did he mean by "seen to it"? What had he done, or ordered to be done? "Ms. Price, stay here a moment and get yourself back together. We'll wait for you downstairs."

Montgomery left and Justine waited, till she heard his footsteps fade away down the corridor. With Blake's safety forefront in her mind, she moved instinctively toward the phone. Just as she touched the receiver, a sense of something wrong filled her body. Her intuition told her not to touch the phone. It would be the wrong thing to do. Slowly, she pulled back her hand, walked to the mirror, touched up her make-up and left to join Montgomery.

Montgomery had met Armon in the library. Armon was sitting at the desk, watching the multi-line phone. "Anything?" Armon shook his head, no. "Not a flicker."

"I'm still not sure. You keep a close eye on her, while we're in Rockham. I want to know everything she does... everything."

"What do you think she's up to?"

"Maybe nothing. Maybe I'm just off because she looks so much like Nora. Or maybe... she's a thief, or DEA, FBI, local Vice. I don't know."

"Why don't you just get rid of her?"

"I think you know the answer to that as well as I do. You see what I see, when I look at her. Watching her with that man affected you as much as it did me. It's like watching a ghost. I want Nora back. She should never have died."

By now, Justine was in the hall and could hear Montgomery talking. "I still can't believe it happened. Nora was always so full of life and so beautiful."

Armon watched Montgomery, with a hatred that came deep from in his soul. The look vanished as Montgomery turned to him. "You keep an eye on her, Armon."

Justine went back to the stairs and made noise, to alert them she had arrived. Montgomery met her in the hall. "Are you alright, now?"

"Yes."

"Pat has brought the car round. The bags are already loaded and the plane is waiting."

Montgomery took her elbow and led her to the car. Armon followed close behind.

The ride was tensely quiet. Justine caught Pat watching through the rear view mirror, whenever possible. It was as if he expected some sort of activity from the back seat. Every muscle in Justine's body was beginning to tighten under the stress and uneasiness that had developed inside her. Montgomery was suspicious. He was doing something about Blake. What was he planning to do about her? Were they going to take her up in the plane and conveniently loose her somewhere between here and Rockham? She felt the outline of the gun in her purse and gained minimal relief. There were two of them and only one of her. Both men were armed. If it came down to a shootout, even Justine's expert marksmanship would be no match for the two of them. Over and over, she reminded herself... they knew nothing. She was as safe as could be expected. Blake would get inside Montgomery's safe, find the evidence, and it would all be over. By the time they flew back from Rockham, it would all be over... maybe even before.

Upon landing in Rockham, they were picked up by a limo, delivered to a luxury hotel downtown, and led to a large suite of rooms on the 5th floor. Justine stood in front of the window, overlooking the sprawling city, as Montgomery placed a call. He seemed disappointed when he replaced the receiver. "Armon." Montgomery's voice was angry. Armon answered from the room he'd chosen, next to Justine's. "Get out of here, Armon."

"Yes, Mr. Montgomery."

"Take Justine out. Take her shopping or sightseeing or whatever. Don't come back till after 8. Go out to dinner, a movie, anything. And I don't want to be disturbed, when you come back." Montgomery went into his own room nearly pulling the door from it's hinges.

Justine's face showed her surprise at the outburst. Armon smiled wryly at her. "You want to change before we go? Something comfortable that you can wear right through dinner?"

"I think I better."

Justine changed into slacks, low heals, and a soft sweater. Armon nodded his approval, then ushered her down the hall and into the elevator. The doors closed. "Did I do something wrong. Is Mr. Montgomery angry with me?"

"It probably has nothing at all to do with you... or me. He gets like this sometimes. When things don't go his way. He just wants to be alone... not be bothered... for a while. Fair warning, though, when we get back tonight... you are liable to find that Mr. Montgomery is no longer alone. You'll hear a lot of... noises coming from his room. Don't worry about it. He'll probably have a couple hookers or some of the local talent in there with him. It's his form of... stress management."

Justine raised her eyebrows and followed Armon from the elevator.

What would be the right word to describe Montgomery... eccentric? Quirky? Weird?

Armon stopped when they reached the lobby. "So, what say we start with lunch here at the hotel?"

"Sounds fine."

Armon ordered lunch and was more talkative than usual with Justine. He seemed more friendly and less staid.

They returned to the lobby, after lunch. "What next? Shopping, sightseeing, a matinee?"

"Since I've never been here before, I'll leave it to you."

"Well, I've never been here before either, but I'll check with the desk clerk. You wait here."

As Justine stood waiting an obviously drunk, middle aged man approached her, coming from the bar. The man was convinced she was a hooker and offered her money. When Justine told him he'd made a mistake and moved away, the man grabbed her arm and became abusive. Armon appeared at Justine's side, his face seething with rage. "Let her go."

The man's speech was slurry. "Why? My money's just as good as yours."

Armon grabbed the man and pushed him hard, up against the wall. He showed the man the gun under his jacket. "I ought to blow your head off, and if you don't leave her alone... I think I will."

The man's face went pale at the sight of the gun, and he fell all over himself with apologies. Armon pushed him one more time, before turning away. Adeptly, Armon pulled himself back together, smoothing his hair and straightening his clothes. "I'm sorry about that. Come on. The clerk told me there is a very exclusive ladies shop, not too far. Mr. Montgomery will be taking us out on the town tomorrow night. You'll need something dynamite to wear."

The more Justine discovered about Armon, the more confused she became. Her original picture of him kept changing, as another facet of his personality slipped to the surface. Armon had many conflicting sides. If Justine hadn't known there was no reason for it, she would have accepted what just happened as a jealous rage on Armon's part. But he had no reason to be jealous.

Justine tried on outfit after outfit, showing them to Armon. He turned everything down, until she appeared in a deep plum, silk dress. He smiled broadly. "Perfect!"

Justine couldn't help thinking, he was harder to please than she was, about clothes. He definitely had a passion for purple. Justine changed and the sales lady packed up her purchases. After the dress shop, they shopped for shoes, and accessories. Finally, Armon pulled Justine into a fur shop. Justine was surprised and listened as Armon spoke to the store clerk. "I want to see something in blue fox. Something soft and uncomplicated."

The clerk nodded and went into the back. "Armon... what are you doing?"

"You have to have a fur. It's still chilly at night."

"But I couldn't possibly, it's... so expensive."

Armon placed his hands on Justine's shoulders. "When Mr. Montgomery goes out in public, he likes to be seen with the very best. So, you must look your very best. He likes to impress people. Trust me."

Armon's boyish face beamed, as if very pleased with himself. Justine did not question him further and tried on the coat. She stood in front of the mirror. It was indeed an elegant piece of work. Justine felt like a princess... like Cinderella... happy yet sad, knowing it all would end very soon. There was nothing that said she couldn't enjoy it while it lasted. She rubbed her cheek against the soft collar.

"It's perfect. I'd like it delivered to this address tomorrow morning." Armon handed the sales clerk a business card, with the address of the hotel and the room number scribbled on the back.

Justine felt herself hating to give up the coat to the clerk. Armon leaned against the counter, his arms folded across his chest, watching Justine. "Are you hungry yet?"

Justine laughed. "I'm too excited to be hungry. The coat is just lovely."

"You should always have nice things."

Why, she couldn't explain, but Justine felt herself blushing, like a school girl. Armon was brought to attention by the color in her cheeks and smiled softly at her. He placed his arm over her shoulders and pulled her close to his side.

"You are very special."

Armon walked her out of the store and onto the sidewalk.

"Mr. Montgomery has a business associate here in town, that owns one of the larger theaters. I'll have him buy out the 5 o'clock show for us. Alright?"

Justine nodded.

"I'll go back inside and call him. Don't wander off."

Justine waited near the door to the shop. She was struck by the feeling she was being watched. Looking across the street, she spotted a man, looking in her direction. At first, she was frightened, but then realized it must be the local Bureau people. Armon returned.

"We have the theater. They are showing a comedy. A good one. I think you'll enjoy it."

They took a cab. When they arrived at the theater, they were escorted into the empty theater and seated. The lights went down and the movie began. It was an eerie feeling, being the only ones in the theater. Once underway, the movie turned out to be every bit as funny as predicted. Justine couldn't help but enjoy it. She had made note, however, that halfway through the film, Armon's arm found it's way around her shoulders. Taking it as a friendly gesture, Justine said nothing. Dinner was equally as enjoyable, as the entire day had been.

Both of them were in a jovial mood when they arrived back at the suite. Armon had correctly warned Justine about what she might find when they returned to the suite. Giddy laughter and waves of passion drifted into the sitting room. Armon whispered to Justine. "Be very quiet. You go ahead to your room."

Justine followed Armon's suggestion, went to her room and changed into her nightgown. She slipped on her robe, when Armon knocked at the door adjoining their rooms. He was holding two glasses of champagne.

"I brought you a nightcap."

"I..."

"Come on. A high class finish to a very high class, very enjoyable day."

Justine smiled and accepted the drink. She placed the glass to her lips and Armon toasted "bottoms up".

Justine obliged, then handed the empty glass back to Armon.

"Pleasant dreams... Ms. Price."

Armon smiled sweetly at her. Justine took little notice of the bitter taste to the drink, until after Armon had left. Dismissing it, she crawled into bed. It had been a busy day. She was very tired.

Armon made himself comfortable and waited, going back to the sitting room and pouring himself another glass of champagne. He stood outside Montgomery's room, listening. The rage that came and went from that dark place inside him, filled his eyes. He downed the drink and poured another, checking the clock. The time ticked by and each click echoed through his mind. As memories of some frightening event flooded his consciousness, he closed his eyes and fell into the chair. He fought back the waves of unpleasant memories and, again checked the time. Thirty minutes had passed since the drink he shared with Justine. It had been long enough. One last drink and he returned to his room. Standing at the door between his room and Justine's, he rapped softly. There was no answer. Slowly, he opened the door and spoke her name. She did not answer. The sleeping pills had taken affect. Justine would not wake till morning.

Armon stood at the side of the bed, looking down at her, his face distorted with a consuming desire. Justine's body lay quiet and peaceful, covered only by the silky pink gown, as he pulled back the covers. He spoke softly as he removed his clothes. "I've missed you so much. We were always special to each other. I've never had another woman. Even after you were gone. There was no one."

Armon's breathing deepened. "If he hadn't messed things up between us, you wouldn't have died. I'm glad you've come back.. But this time... I'll make sure he doesn't have you. I've got a plan. I'm going to fix it so we can always be together."

Armon climbed into bed beside Justine. Trembling, he ran his hand over her cheek, down her neck and on to her body. He kissed her face and whispered. "I'll make sure he doesn't have you. You belong to me, now... and forever."

Chapter 7

Justine felt strange when she woke. She wrote if off to the activity of the previous day, showered and dressed. Armon had already ordered breakfast for the two of them. Mr. Montgomery was still sleeping. "Did you sleep well?"

"Yes, Armon. Thank you. And thank you for a fun day yesterday."

"I made an appointment for you... 2 o'clock to have your hair done."

Justine looked questioningly at him. "We are going out this evening. You need a hairdo, to go with the new clothes." Armon smiled.

Justine smiled back. It was hard to keep sight of her purpose.

Mr. Montgomery appeared at his door, just as Armon was pushing the breakfast table into the hall. Armon closed the door, then turned to Mr. Montgomery. "Would you like breakfast?"

"No. Just have them send up a large pot of coffee."

Armon ordered the coffee.

"Ms. Price, I have some things I'd like you to do today. Get your notebook."

Justine went to her room and returned, with the notebook and a pencil. Montgomery ran down a long list of phone calls he wanted made... two people she was to see and collect information packets from... and she and Armon were to collect a Mr. Alberto Arroro at the airport at 4:30.

Mr. Montgomery expected to be gone most of the day. "Oh, and we'll all be dining out tonight. High class. Pick up something appropriate to wear."

Justine smiled at Armon. "Yes, Mr. Montgomery."

The coffee arrived and Montgomery took it to his room, closing the door.

Justine went to the desk and started the phone calls.

By 10, the calls were completed, and she phoned the desk and requested a cab. She hadn't expected Armon would be going with her, but found him trotting along behind her to the elevator. "Are you coming with me?"

"Can't have you wandering around a strange city all by yourself. Besides, I have to make sure you get back here in time to make your hair appointment."

"I'd forgotten about that."

"See there, you need your own secretary."

Justine could hardly comprehend the drastic change in Armon. He was a different person. There was no way Justine could know just how changed Armon was. They picked up the packets and made it back to the hotel in time for lunch. Justine noted that the fox fur had arrived in their absence. She pulled it from the box and lay it across the bed, excited to know she would soon be wearing it. Armon called her out of the bedroom. "You better get to your appointment. I'll meet you back up here, to go to the airport."

Justine agreed and went to the salon.

As she sat in the chair waiting for the next phase of the process, a woman came and sat near her. The woman spoke to Justine, without looking at her. "Justine Edwards?"

"Yes." Justine followed the woman's lead and did not look directly at her.

"Do you have any information?"

"I'm picking up a man at the airport at 4:30. He sounds South American. I don't have anything specific about him. I have a feeling that Montgomery is handling the real deal. I think he's been running me around."

"You think he suspects?"

"I'm not sure."

The woman started to leave.

"Wait. Is everything... alright on the outside? Blake Hampton... have you heard anything about him?"

"No. Nothing. I've got to go."

There was still that nagging fear inside Justine that something had happened to Blake. Something must have happened or she'd have heard from him... by now.

Justine and Armon waited, as Mr. Arroro's bags were checked through. Justine introduced herself and Armon, then escorted Mr. Arroro to a waiting limo. A suite of rooms had already been reserved for Mr. Arroro at the hotel. They settled him in, then went back to their suite. Mr. Montgomery had not yet returned.

"I've made dinner reservations for 8. You go ahead and do whatever you have to do, to be ready. I'll hold the fort."

Justine smiled back at Armon. He had become so considerate and attentive, since they landed in Rockham. It was getting hard to keep him in perspective. All this attention however, was probably just a ruse to allow him to keep a close eye on her.

Justine showered, put on her evening make-up and dressed. She was ready by 7 on the dot. Armon had changed and was waiting in the sitting room. He was struck dumb by the sight of Justine, in the plum dress, her hair swept back away from her face, carrying the fox fur over her arm. "Armon, are you alright?"

"Uh... yeah. Just seeing it all together is... I did a good job."

"You have excellent taste, Armon."

"I used to get a lot of practice. I picked out all my mother's clothes... she thought I had good taste too."

"I hope Mr. Montgomery will be satisfied with it. Is he back?"

"Yes, he's changing. He'll be out in a minute or two. And... I'm sure he'll be satisfied. I'm sure. How about a glass of champagne to start the evening?" Armon was already pouring the drink.

"No. I don't think I'd better."

Armon shrugged. "As you wish."

Mr. Montgomery stepped from his room, looking severely elegant in his evening clothes. His eyes fell on Justine, then flashed to Armon, who was smiling like the Cheshire cat. Justine expected a compliment or at least a word of approval. There was none. "We better collect Mr. Arroro and get going. I don't want to be late."

Mr. Montgomery led the way out the door and down the hall to Mr. Arroro's room. He knocked loudly and Mr. Arroro answered, equally as elegantly dressed. His thick accent was difficult to understand. "Mr. Montgomery."

"Mr. Arroro. Shall we get the evening underway?"

"I see you have provided me with a lovely escort this evening, Mr. Montgomery." Mr. Arroro was gazing eagerly at Justine.

"No, Mr. Arroro. The lady you requested is waiting in the lobby."

"What a pity. But then, I can see why you would want to keep her to yourself." Mr. Arroro took Justine's hand and kissed it.

"You will at least allow her to accompany me to the lobby?"

Montgomery's collar appeared too tight. He didn't smile, when he answered. "Of course, Mr. Arroro. Of course."

Mr. Arroro took Justine's arm and held her quite close to him in the elevator. As they approached the lobby, Mr. Arroro's hand managed to slip from Justine's arm, around her back and under her arm, to cup her breast.

Reactively, Justine moved away from him, in an offended manner. Mr. Arroro laughed out loud. "I see she is a lady, Mr. Montgomery. Does she protest as much with you?"

Montgomery made no response, as none was expected. Instead, he engaged Mr. Arroro in polite conversation, as Armon moved between Arroro and Justine. There again in

Armon's eyes, was that rage which, to Justine, was out of place. Once in the lobby, they were joined by an attractive young blonde and an equally attractive brunette. The introductions were made. However, when Mr. Montgomery indicated that Armon would be escorting the young brunette, Armon flashed an angry look at Montgomery, then let it die and took the young woman's arm.

It became increasingly evident that there would be no business discussed between Mr. Montgomery and Mr. Arroro. This evening was strictly for entertainment. This fact reinforced Justine's theory, that Arroro was not the connection. As the evening wore on, Mr. Arroro's state of intoxication, became more and more abhorrent. Finally Montgomery suggested they return to his suite and continue the evening there. Arroro agreed, much to the relief of the establishment's management.

Back at the hotel, Montgomery ordered drinks and food, then went to his room to change. At some point during the evening, a VCR and some videos had been set up in the room. Montgomery cranked down the lights, then popped a tape into the machine. Mr. Arroro seated himself at the best vantage point, with his little blonde tucked under one arm and Armon's brunette under the other. Mr. Montgomery smiled at seeing Arroro become absorbed in the movie. He walked toward Armon, who was standing off to the side, and whispered to him. "Get everything set up in Arroro's room. I'll have him over there in about a half hour."

Armon nodded, slipped a sidelong glance at Justine, then left the room.

It was obvious to Justine that they were setting Mr. Arroro up... for something. Just what that something was, could be anyone's guess. Justine was at a loss about what she was expected to do, so she approached Mr. Montgomery. "If you don't need me for anything else, Mr. Montgomery..."

"Don't go to bed just yet. Change if you like, but come back out here."

Justine went to her room and changed into a more casual attire. When she returned, she found Mr. Montgomery sitting in a chair, near Mr. Arroro. Arroro was wholly lost in the sexual exploits parading across the screen. Having no real interest in watching, Justine crossed to the bar and made herself a drink. Montgomery joined her. He spoke to her in low tones.

"Whatever I say or do, just go along with it. Don't react to what I do or say. Alright?"

Justine was concerned about what Mr. Montgomery had in mind, but agreed.

"Come and sit with me."

Montgomery took Justine by the hand and led her back to the chair, pulling her down on his lap. His reappearance in the chair, with Justine, caught Arroro's attention. Montgomery knew Arroro was watching, but pretended not to see him. Montgomery ran his hand up Justine's thigh, over her hip and up to her back. Then, he pushed her back into his arm and began kissing her face and neck. Justine closed her eyes. She hoped Montgomery had some plan and this wasn't just a play for her body. He pushed the loose fitting top off Justine's shoulder, baring her soft pale flesh.

Arroro became intent, taking a large gulp of his drink and wiping the residue from his mouth with his hand. He was little more than a drunken pig.

As Arroro watched, Montgomery moved his hand up under Justine's top, exposing the smooth flesh of her abdomen. The brunette on Arroro's right left the room, followed by the blonde. Arroro was totally unaware that the girls had left. The girls gone, Montgomery pretended to notice Arroro was watching.

"Mr. Arroro, what happened to the ladies?"

Arroro looked around, decidedly surprised. He leapt to his feet, as well as could be expected, in his drunken condition. "What is this? You promised me a special woman tonight."

"And I delivered. I can't help it if you couldn't keep even one of them. There were two you know."

Arroro reached out for Justine. "Then I'll take this one."

Montgomery intercepted Arroro's reach. "No, Mr. Arroro. This one is mine. I must ask you to leave, now."

Arroro was furious. Montgomery had intentionally frustrated the man to near insanity, but why? Arroro did not close the door behind him.

Montgomery pushed Justine from his lap, but kept a firm grip on her wrist. He held her in tow, as he walked to the door and watched to be sure Arroro made it inside his suite.

Smiling like the fox with feathers in his teeth, Montgomery closed the door and turned to Justine. "We did it."

"Did what?"

"Nothing you need to know about."

Montgomery tilted his head to the side and scrutinized Justine. "You know... you're handier to have around than Paul. I might just have to fire him."

Montgomery raised his eyebrows and smiled. "Ah, but then I might never get you into my bed."

Montgomery's face took on another expression, more soft and genuine. "You looked very elegant this evening." Montgomery still held her wrist. He pulled her in close to him, placing his other hand aside her face. Justine knew what was coming. Montgomery had frustrated himself, as well as Mr. Arroro.

Her situation was dangerous, now. The wrong word, the wrong movement and she would be under assault. "Mr. Montgomery, I'm very tired. May I be excused now... please?"

Justine kept her tone steady and low, trying not to show fearfulness.

"Yes. You're right." Montgomery sighed deeply. "I have some things to see to. You go on to bed."

Montgomery managed a small smile, but there was pain in his face. As soon as he let go, Justine turned and fled to the small safety of her room.

She lay awake a long time, listening and waiting, too frightened to sleep. She heard Armon return, just before dawn. She listened at the door, but their voices were too muffled. Upon hearing Armon enter his room, Justine dashed back to the bed. The door between the two rooms opened and Armon stepped into the room. She felt him standing close, near the bed. Then he spoke... in a whisper.

"Don't worry... I won't let anything happen to you. I won't let him hurt you. It will all be over soon." He bent over and kissed her on the cheek.

Justine wanted to leap from the bed, but was luckily, too petrified to do so. Armon left the room and the door closed. Justine's eyes opened and her lungs gasped for oxygen. This was getting very complicated. But it would be over soon... over soon, she knew. But what did Armon know?

Armon roused Justine after barely four hours sleep. "Get up sleepy head. We're going home."

"What?"

"We're leaving. Get dressed and pack your things."

Justine shook her head in an attempt to break Morpheus' hold on her brain. "Leaving..." She mumbled to herself. "Get dressed and get packed... right."

Instead of a limo, they used a rented car to return to the airstrip. Armon hustled Justine onto the plane, then returned to Mr. Montgomery, near the car.

Soon, another car appeared on the strip. A tall Latin man emerged and two armed men. Mr. Montgomery, briefcase in hand, walked toward the Latin's car. The trunk was opened and the two men examined it's contents. They seemed to come to some agreement and the two armed men removed the packages from the trunk and loaded them onto the plane.

Meanwhile, the Latin examined the contents of the brief-case. This was it. The buy was happening right here, in front of her. All she could do was be witness to it. The plane's engine's started up, then Justine heard what, at first, she thought was a car back-firing. Men with automatic weapons ran from the woods, toward the airstrip. Justine wasn't sure whether they were officials or a rival group trying to take the bundles.

She grabbed for the gun in her purse. It was gone.

Justine watched and hoped. Armon snatched the briefcase from the Latin and ran toward the plane. As he reached the top step, he yelled to the pilot to take off, pulling up the gangway. Bullets flew from every direction.

Justine prayed they wouldn't blow up the plane with her aboard. She wasn't ready to die, not yet. The plane lifted from the runway and the shots faded. Justine was visibly shaken. Armon stood in the isle, laughing.

"We did it! We got the money, we got the dope, and we're rid of him. We're set for life. We can go anywhere we want, do anything we want. We're rich! No more trashy movies for you, mother. No more putting up with what little bit they hand out. He'll never put his hands on you again."

Armon came to a dumbfounded Justine and sat beside her. He took her hands in his. "You see mom, just like I promised. I'll take care of you. It's just you and me again. Just like it used to be."

Justine tried to remain calm, in the face of the fact that Armon had gone off the deep end. He was convinced she was his mother. Think! She had to think. One of the engines started to sputter. The pilot yelled back for Armon. Armon kissed Justine, patted her hand, then joined the pilot.

Justine saw Armon hand the pilot two large bundles of cash, then he rejoined her. "We took some damage. The pilot is going to set us down, as soon as he thinks it's safe."

"What happened back there, Armon?"

"I thought it was really quite clever of me. I let the DEA know where the buy was to take place. I told them to wait Till the plane was loaded and the briefcase transferred. I figured that would give me enough time to get in a position to grab the case and get to the plane... before either of them knew what hit them. Didn't I do a good job, mother?"

"Yes, Armon. But now they'll be looking for you... and for me."

"No they won't. The pilot is going to set us down, take the plane back up, parachute out and blow it up. We'll all be dead. They won't be looking for any of us... or the money... or the dope."

Justine realized that though warped, Armon's thinking was diabolical. His plan would very likely work. It would look good for the politicians to have Montgomery behind bars. Even without the drugs, they might very well have him on murder. Montgomery was shooting at the DEA men and some of them went down. The drugs and others involved would be destroyed. Case closed. No one looking for him... and no one looking for her.

Armon laughed. "I bet Montgomery is really pissed, after going to all that trouble to set Arroro up for future use. I've got the blackmail tape, along with everything else."

"What did he do to Arroro?"

"The same thing he did to all the others. Set him up for an embarrassing, blackmailable, situation and taped the whole thing. You saw how Mr. Montgomery got Arroro all worked up with the booze and the girls and the video. The man was ripe for the picking. When Arroro went to his room... there was a maid there. A nice sexy little maid. You know... the part you played... the victim. Arroro was so far gone... he jumped her almost the minute he saw her. Got a little carried away though. Montgomery couldn't have been happier. Arroro killed her. It's all on video tape. He was so flipped out from the little extra in his drink, he didn't even know he'd done it. But it was rape... and murder, just the same."

Armon's eyes lit up with a strange pleasure, as he described everything Arroro had done to the poor dead girl. There was something about what Justine was now seeing in Armon, that frightened her more than his twisted mind thinking she was his mother. There was a sense that he could watch a murder... maybe even participate in one, and not be horrified. The innocent youthfulness of his face had vanished over the past few minutes. It took on the hardness of someone who could kill for the pleasure of it and revel in watching others do the same. Her only hope would be to escape him, once they were on the ground.

The pilot set them down in a large field bordered by a dense forest. Justine stepped from the plane with only the fox fur and her purse. Armon pulled the bundles from the plane and signaled the pilot to take off. Justine examined her position. This was not the place to try to get away. Too much open space and Armon was armed.

"Here, you carry the briefcase, mother. Follow me."

Justine followed a few steps behind Armon, until they reached the trees. "We have to find a place to hide this. We can't be traveling around with it." Armon was referring to the bundles.

After looking around, he located a large oak tree. Then, taking a stick from the ground, he began to dig a hole at its base. As soon as the hole was large enough, he dropped the bundles in and covered them over, being careful to spread the leaves back over the spot. He took out his pocket knife and began to carve some letters on the tree, inside a large heart. "ND loves AD". "Only you and I know where it is."

Armon marked the spot on the map from his pocket. "I saw a farm over that way, as we were landing. Let's go."

It was twilight as they approached the rear of the farmhouse. Justine prayed there would be no one at home. Knowing Armon was capable of killing and knowing he wanted to keep their being alive secret, she was sure he would kill anyone who might link them to the area.

Justine's prayers were answered. No one was home. Armon jimmied the door. Without hesitation, he gathered food from the kitchen, filling a pillowcase he collected on the way inside. While Armon was busy, Justine took the coded beeper from her purse, set it, and placed it on the wall phone. It was dark now, and there were places to hide. Now was her chance.

Justine backed away from Armon, toward the door. Armon turned, quickly, somehow sensing her fear and plot to escape him. She stopped cold, as he turned his eyes on her. "Mother... don't do this to me. Don't leave me, again."

Aware of it or not, Armon stood, revolver drawn, aimed directly at her.

"I was just making sure no one was coming."

Armon relaxed. "Oh." He replaced the revolver and took Justine's arm. "We have enough. We better get going." Armon pulled her outside and back towards the wood.

They stopped well beyond the edge of the wood, once the lights of the farmhouse were just twinkles in the dark. "We'll stay here tonight. Can't travel in the dark."

Armon sat down and switched on the small portable radio he'd taken from the farmhouse. Exhausted, Justine collapsed near a tree. Armon tuned to a local station and left it play softly, until the news began to broadcast. He turned the volume up.

The announcer's voice was clear and distinct. "The big news today was the drug bust that took place at a small airstrip just west of Rockham. Authorities have not released the names of persons involved as yet, because there seems to be some confusion over identities. Though the plane loaded with the drugs did manage to lift off the field. It was damaged and later exploded in the country side, over Backfield County, killing all aboard."

Armon turned off the radio. "Yahoo! We did it!"

"Yes, we certainly did. Armon, where are we going?" Justine needed to know where she was.

Armon pulled the map out of his vest pocket and a penlight from his jacket. "From the looks of the map, if we head east, out of here, we should be able to pick up a main road, hitch a ride to Richmond, then take us a nice little boat ride to Florida. I know I can make a deal for the stuff down there... after it cools off, of course. I've got all this money. We'll buy us the biggest, fanciest boat we can find."

Armon came to sit beside Justine. He put his arm around her, then pulled her down to lie beside him on the leaf covered ground. "It's like it used to be, mother. You and me... together. Aren't the stars bright tonight? The whole world seems better, with you back in my life."

Armon pulled her close against his body. "I know I'm the only one you ever really loved. The others... my father, Montgomery, all of them... I know you only did what they wanted, to help me... to give me a life. But I don't like life... without you. I was so lonely. I'd rather be dead. I know that now... now that I see again, what it's like to have you."

Armon turned his head to face her. There was barely an inch between them. "You do love me best don't you, mother? Tell me you love me."

"I love you, Armon." Justine tried not to tremble.

Chapter 8

When the DEA report came down about the scheduled drug bust, Blake was in the hospital having his ribs taped. Someone had taken great pains to hurt him, just enough. It was a professional job. Blake was angry with himself for allowing it to happen. He should have seen it coming. As it was, he made it to the airstrip just in time to see the plane lift off the runway. But he was one of the first at the site of the explosion. No one could have known why this particular case caused him so much pain. Sure, it was hard to loose a fellow agent, but this particular agent was more than a temporary partner... more than badge number 276857... much more.

Blake was directed back to Wilson Falls, to help the team going through Montgomery's estate. The head investigator for the region, Todd Markum, was sitting in front of the TV screen in Montgomery's apartment, when Blake walked in.

"Hello, Todd."

"Blake."

Todd switched off the video. "I'm sorry about your partner. She was very pretty."

"Yeah, she was..." Blake changed the subject. " What you watching... dirty movies?"

Blake's joke was half hearted.

Todd thought a moment, before he responded. "Well, Blake, you're going to find out about it sooner or later. I guess better now."

Todd switched the video back on, to a scene of intimate lovemaking between Montgomery and... Justine.

Blake turned all his attention to the video. He, too, at first, thought he was seeing Justine. But there it was, the proof it wasn't Justine. "Hold that frame Todd."

Todd pressed the pause on the remote control. "What is it, Blake?"

"That's not Justine..."

"What?"

"That's Nora Dupree. See there... on the table near the bed. The haircombs. There was one just like it in Nora's hair, when her body was found. Justine gave me the other one. She found it here on the grounds. Run it back a few frames."

Todd ran the video back, until Blake told him to stop. "There. See that birthmark on her shoulder..."

"Yeah."

"Justine doesn't ... didn't have one."

Todd looked surprised at finding Blake knew Justine so intimately.

"You don't have to spread it around, Todd. Just take my word for it, that's not Justine. Little difference it makes now, though." Blake turned sullen and quiet.

A young man appeared in the doorway. "Mr. Markum, I think you better come see this."

Todd looked at Blake, shrugged, then both men followed the younger one down the hall.

The young man showed them into a bedroom, near the end of the hall. The room was the color of a giant plum... Purple everything... everywhere. The walls of the room were covered with photographs... of Justine... or Nora... or both. Todd was confused. "Which one of them is this, Blake?"

Blake examined the pictures, closely. "Some of these are older than the others. I'd say the older ones were Nora and the newer ones were Justine."

Blake removed one of the pictures from the wall. "It's amazing how much they looked alike." Blake lost himself in the photograph, until the young man spoke again.

"That's not all; the guy kept a diary. If Nora Dupree was his mother, they were both pretty sick. You should read this stuff. The last entries get real confusing. It looks like he couldn't tell the difference between the two of them either. The guy must have been whacko."

Blake took the diary from the young man and skimmed through it as he spoke to Todd. "Have you questioned the staff?"

"They're talking to the housekeeper now, downstairs."

"I'd like to talk to her."

"Be my guest."

The housekeeper was sitting at the kitchen table, tearful and obviously frightened. Todd motioned for the man doing the questioning to get up from the chair and allow Blake to take over. "Ma'am, you have nothing to be afraid of if you cooperate with us. We already have Montgomery in custody and he won't be getting out anytime soon. Any information you can give us will be appreciated."

The housekeeper blotted her eyes and nodded that she understood. "What can you tell me about Nora Dupree's murder?"

The woman broke down, again.

"Please, ma'am. We need your help." Blake motioned for Todd and the other man to leave the room.

"Ma'am, we are not out to convict you of anything. Montgomery is the one we wanted and we have him. We just want to get a clear picture... and the more information we can tie together, the better we'll know how to keep him where he is."

"Alright. What do you want to know about Nora?"

"Was she killed here?"

The woman nodded. "Yes, in the cottage."

"Did you see him do it?"

"No, I only heard her screaming. By the time I got there she was dead."

"What happened, then?"

"He threatened me. Told me he'd do the same to me, if I told anyone about it. He took her out of the cottage and put her body round the back, TILL he could get his car out there. He put her in the trunk and took her away. I don't know where. I had to clean it all up... so no one would know... so much blood."

Mrs. Gibson was on a roll now. "When that woman came here... Ms. Price... I like ta died of freight. I could have sworn it was Nora... back from the dead. Mr. Montgomery saw it right away, so did Armon... and Pat, the grounds manager. I was so afraid the same thing was going to happen all over, again. Every time I went to that cottage, I felt sick. I could see the hate come up in his eyes, every time he saw them together. He was a very sick boy. He and his mother were unnatural... you know... perverse. They slept together.

"She was real young, when she had Armon. She lived a real rough life. Men weren't good to her. Armon started taking care of her when he was a small child. Her being abused so much. I guess he saw so many men abuse her... it was just a part of him. Montgomery tried to help her... take care of her. I truly think they loved each other. But Armon... he hated it. He was jealous you see... like a lover. That's how he happened to kill her... in a jealous rage. He made her confess all sorts of things... he kept hurting her... then he just squeezed the life right out of her. I could hear it as I was running across the lawn. I still hear it in my nightmares. You're sure Armon is dead?"

"Wait a minute. Are you telling me Armon Dupree killed his mother? It wasn't Preston Montgomery?"

"No! Armon killed her! Mr. Montgomery never knew who did it. I think he suspected, maybe, but he never said anything."

Blake was stunned. He'd been way off base. He'd been looking at the case straight on instead of askew. It was a sick twisted mess. Blake's stomach churned to think how much danger Justine had been in. She wasn't up against a cold blooded killer, she was up against a psychopath.

"I was real sorry to hear that nice young woman was killed. She didn't understand what was going on. She asked me about it once. I almost told her, but Armon came in..."

"Thank you. You can tell the rest to the investigator. I'll send him back in."

Blake left the room, sending the investigator back to Mrs. Gibson. He stood with Todd in the hall. "Todd, how could I have been so off the mark? Armon killed his own mother! He was never even a suspect. Damn!"

The phone in the library rang. Todd answered. He looked surprised by the call, took the information, hung up, then turned to Blake. "Blake, you aren't going to believe this. Control is receiving a transmission from the coded beeper Justine was assigned... from a phone in Backfield County. The office thinks there is a possibility the beeper may have been picked up from the wreckage of the plane and accidentally switched on... They want me to send someone down there... you want to go?"

"You're damn right I do. Give me the information."

Todd handed the slip of paper to Blake. As Blake turned to leave, Todd grabbed his arm. "Blake... I had no idea there was anything between you and Justine... don't get your hopes up. This could be nothing." Todd smiled understandingly at Blake. "But, I hope she is still alive. Good luck."

"Thanks, Todd. Notify the local authorities I'm on my way down. I'll need their help to find this place." Todd nodded and Blake rushed from the house.

At the airport, Blake commandeered a charter plane to fly him to Rockham. He was met by the State Police and driven to the Backfield sheriff's office. The sheriff was out, but the deputy gave them directions to the farm.

They arrived to find the sheriff, arriving just ahead of them. The owner of the house was standing on the porch, awaiting the sheriff. The sheriff approached the State Police car, as Blake and the trooper stepped out.

"I don't remember callin' in the State Police. What's goin' on?"

The trooper explained that Blake was with the Bureau and that a signal had been received through this phone, on the coded beeper of one of their agents.

"Well don't know nothin 'bout that, I'm here to investigate a break in. Well, you come along inside with me. We'll see what we can see."

Blake and the trooper followed the sheriff and an hysterical woman inside the house. Blake went straight to the phone.

The beeper wasn't there. "Excuse me, ma'am. Did you find some little black box near the phone? Looks like a calculator."

"Yeah. It's out on the picnic table. I thought it was a bomb or something."

Blake stepped out the back door, retrieved the beeper and returned. "Excuse me, again, ma'am. Did you find this right on the phone?"

"Yes. I did."

"May I use your phone?"

"I guess so."

Blake placed a collect call to Mr. Compson, on his private number. "Harold, it's Blake... I'm down in Backfield County... I've got Justine's beeper... No... it wasn't just accidental. It was placed right on the phone. Only Justine would know to do that... From the looks of things here, she's not alone. She's either with the pilot or Armon Dupree or both of them... Yes... yes... the explosion was a fake and the drugs are probably still floating around. What really worries me is, if Justine is with Armon Dupree, she's in a lot of trouble she doesn't know about. Talk to Todd. He'll explain. I want to stay down here... You better have them set up road blocks along the North Carolina, Virginia boarder. That's the only logical direction they would take from here."

On the other end of the line Mr. Compson agreed with Blake's logic, indicating that their questioning of Montgomery had revealed the possibility that Armon might try to get to the Virginia shore and pick up a boat to Florida.

"I'll check in every four hours. If you get anything, get in touch through the State Police... Thanks."

Blake hung up and turned to the sheriff. "Sheriff, it will be light soon. You have tracking dogs available?"

"The best in the county."

"You think you could have them here by first light?"

"No problem."

The sheriff went to his car, used the radio, then came back inside. Blake asked that both departments keep everything quiet, so not to endanger the agent's life. All involved agreed that was the right way to go.

Men began arriving with tracking dogs, just before the sun broke the horizon. It didn't take long for the dogs to pick up on the direction of the fugitive. The noise from the dogs reached Armon and Justine, already well on their way to the main road. Armon was cautious about the sound of the dogs, but not overly concerned. The noise from traveling vehicles was nearer than the dogs. Armon took Justine by the arms.

"When we get to the road, you get a car to stop. Then I'll come up."

"You won't hurt anyone, will you, Armon?"

Armon shrugged. "Not unless they try to hurt us."

Justine climbed up onto the roadway. Two cars passed, then one stopped. The driver leaned over and popped open the passenger's door. By the time he turned back to the wheel, Armon had the driver's door open and the gun to the man's head.

"Now, I don't want to hurt you. Put it in park and scoot over. Get in, Mom."

Justine climbed in next to the man, and Armon slid behind the wheel. She had considered running, but Armon would definitely have killed the driver if she did.

With one hand on the gun and the other gripping the wheel, Armon turned off the main road and down onto a dirt road. He parked the car near some trees and got out. He ordered the man out of the car and made him walk off the road into the trees.

When Justine heard the shot, she slid under the wheel hoping for escape. Armon had blocked that avenue by taking the keys. She slid back to the passenger's side, as Armon returned to the car. "Armon... you said you wouldn't hurt anyone."

"But I had to, mother. No one can know we're alive. You understand don't you?"

Justine was having difficulty holding off hysterics. She had never felt so helpless and alone. She was angry with herself. She should be able to handle this situation. Armon put the car back into gear, turned around, and drove back to the main road. Justine could hardly think straight. She had to get away from him, somehow.

"Armon, could we stop at the next gas station. I have to go to the bathroom."

"Yeah, I need some gas anyway."

Armon pulled into a small country store/gas station combination. He stopped Justine, before she got out of the car. "Remember, don't do anything to make them remember you, or I'll have to kill them. And, don't try to run away."

Armon's eyes left no doubt in Justine's mind that he would kill anyone who crossed him. "Alright, I'll remember."

Justine went inside and asked for the key to the ladies room. Once inside the ladies room, Justine locked the door and leaned across the sink, sure she was going to be ill. Her mind was reeling. How could she get free of him, without endangering innocent people? She looked up at herself in the mirror. She could write on the mirror... but Armon might come in after her and check. Through the mirror, she could see the open stall door behind her. It was covered with graffiti. Who would notice one more piece of graffiti, except maybe the store owners. Taking her lipstick from her purse, Justine wrote the word CASCADE in big letters on the inside of the stall wall. It looked like one more piece of graffiti. It wouldn't mean anything to Armon... but on the slim chance the Bureau had any idea which way they'd gone... it would mean something to them... to Blake... if he was still alive.

As an after thought, Justine removed a 50 dollar bill from her wallet and, using the lipstick, wrote the word CASCADE

94

across its face. She folded it neatly and tucked it back in her purse. Armon was finishing pumping the gas, when she returned. "You want me to pay for the gas?"

Armon smiled. "Yeah. But cash only."

Justine nodded and went inside the store. She handed the lady behind the counter the key and the folded fifty dollar bill, telling her to keep the change.

"Well, thank you, ma'am. You all come, again, real soon."

Justine returned to the car. Armon came back from the directions of the rest rooms and slid behind the wheel. He patted her hand on the seat. "That was real good, mom. It will all work out fine. You'll see."

Armon headed the car up the road toward, what Justine was seeing as, an uncertain future.

The state and local authorities were concentrating their efforts from the main road east, since the dogs lost the trail. Jimmy Coburn, part-time deputy, part-time fireman, part-time rancher, taking the day off to go fishing, stopped in to have a talk with Mrs. Dehaven, drop her a fish or two, and get some gas on his way home. He hadn't heard about all the excitement. But he did think it a bit curious, when Mrs. Dehaven told him about the 50 dollar bill, with the word CASCADE across its face in lipstick.

Mrs. Dehaven handed it to him.

"If that don't beat all."

"You don't think it's counterfeit or anything do you, Jimmy?"

"Couldn't rightly say Mrs. Dehaven. If you like, I'll check with Mr. Potter at the bank, first thing Monday morning."

"Thank you, Jimmy. I sure would appreciate it."

"It's probably nothing, just a prank of some kind. You know we get some strange birds through here, during the tourist season."

Jimmy folded the bill along the creases and tucked it into his pocket. "See 'ya Monday, Mrs. Dehaven."

"Bye, Jimmy."

Mrs. Dehaven locked the door behind Jimmy. She always closed at 1 on Saturday.

With each passing hour, Justine became more and more convinced that no one would ever find her. Having had little sleep the night before and knowing she could not think clearly being overtired, she folded the blue fox fur into a pillow between Armon and herself. Then, knowing no other option, lay her head upon the coat. She felt fairly confident that Armon would not harm her while she slept. The motion of the car lulled her weary brain into a fitful sleep.

By the time she woke, Armon had already stopped, again, for gas and was pulling out of the station. "Damn." She thought to herself. She'd missed an opportunity.

Armon smiled over at her, as she sat up.

"Feel better now?"

"Yes."

"Sit over here, next to me."

Justine wanted to keep Armon happy and calm, so she did as he asked and slid next to him. He wrapped his arm around her and pushed her head down on his shoulder. "We are going to be so happy together. Just the two of us. When you first showed up at Montgomery's, I wasn't sure it was you. He told me you were dead. But that night... in Rockham... when I lay with you in bed..."

Justine lifted her head. "What night?"

"That's right. You wouldn't remember that. I'm sorry I had to do that. I put you to sleep... but I had to be sure it was you. I had to feel you close to my body... to know it was you. I got the idea from the time Montgomery had you knock that guy out to make the blackmail video, with those three teenyboppers. But boy I'm sure and I'll never have to put you to sleep, again. I'd rather have you looking at me and kissing me back. I like it much better that way. You are the perfect lover, mother." He squeezed her close.

Justine sat, in shock, with no sense of time. This young boy, barely a man, had violated her. He had a sick distorted relationship with his mother. And, now, he was convinced she was his mother. He would expect her to love him, not only through affectionate touching, but through the physical

96

act, as well. How had this happened? How had she become lost in this nightmare... that could only end badly?

Armon slowed the car and pulled to the side. Up ahead a police road block waited. The flashing lights drew Justine out of herself. She grabbed the door handle. All she could think was to run toward the flashing light.

Armon grabbed her arm. "It's OK mother. They haven't seen us. We'll just go another way."

Justine tried to think... to convince him to go on. "How, silly, Armon. They aren't looking for us. We can just drive right through."

"They aren't looking for us... but maybe for the car. We'll head back and take a side road."

Justine watched out the back window, as her hope faded from view.

The car swerved off the main road onto a less traveled back road that led up into the hills. As they traveled higher and higher, and the road became steeper and steeper, the old car began to have trouble making the hills.

Armon became agitated with the car and vowed they would get another... faster, newer car as soon as possible. The road twisted and turned and hilled and valleyed until Justine became ill. She made Armon stop, stumbled from the car, and off the side of the road. It was more than just the ride that was making her sick. A sense of desperation flooded her body in gigantic waves. The time wasn't right, neither was the place, but she couldn't stand it anymore.

Armon was still sitting in the car, looking at the map. Slowly, Justine walked further into the woods. She came to the top of a small hill. The sight below, gave her renewed hope.

With one last glance back, she tore off, full speed, down the hill. A small town sprawled out below her. The closer she got, the more her heart pounded. He knew she was missing now. He would be after her. She couldn't look back. The town seemed deserted. These little towns closed up early on the weekend, but there was a beacon of hope in the darkness... A telephone booth.

Justine fumbled with her purse, as she continued to run toward the booth. Finding a quarter, she pressed every ounce of strength into her legs. She was near hysteria as she grasped the door handle and stepped inside. Shakily, she picked up the receiver and dropped in the quarter. It seemed to take an eternity before the operator came on the line.

"Operator... this is an emergency. I need to place a collect call to 202-555-4343. Please hurry."

Justine realized she'd made a mistake. That was her number at the Bureau. It was Saturday. No one would answer it.

"Operator... operator. Forget that number." Justine's mind was a whirlwind of numbers... which one... which one. Finally, she remembered the number for Emergency Operations. Anxiously, she gave the operator the new number and waited.

At first, she was speechless, when the call was accepted and connected. "State your operation code, please." The voice was speaking to her, but she couldn't remember what to say. What was the code? She knew it... "Your operation code, please."

"Cascade... cascade..."

"State the nature of your emergency."

Armon was behind her in the booth. He took the receiver from her hand and replaced it. There wasn't an ounce of strength or resistance left in her body. She went limp, when his hands touched her and her mind went black.

Chapter 9

Justine woke to find herself in a bed, inside a small cabin. Armon was standing over her. "You slept a long time. You really were sick. Was that what you were trying to do... call a doctor?"

Justine grasped his excuse. "Yes... that was it."

"You didn't need a doctor. Just some good solid sleep. You know how easily you get overtired."

"Where are we?"

"We are in Virginia!" Armon showed his pleasure in his face. "I got another car... a good fast one... and we crossed over last night. It's Sunday. Do you remember what we always used to do on Sunday?"

Justine waited for him to tell her. "You know. We'd have a big breakfast, then take a long walk, and talk about what we would do when we were rich. Remember?"

Justine nodded.

"Well, I've got breakfast all ready. Come on." Armon assisted Justine from the bed, to the table.

Remembering Armon was a good cook, Justine found herself anxious to eat. She was very hungry.

"I bought you a change of clothes. Some jeans and sneakers. They ought to look real wild with your blue fox fur, huh!"

Justine managed a weak smile at his humor. Armon jumped up from the table, and pulled a shirt from the bag on the counter. "Look at this shirt!"

The shirt was his favorite color... purple. Across the front were the words "I'M IN LOVE". Armon wrapped his arms around Justine. "I do love you. I'll never love anyone else."

Looking into this young man's eyes, Justine could believe that he genuinely loved his mother. But the line between love and hate was frail, especially in a confused mind. Justine was not consoled by his profession of love.

"Get changed and we'll go for our walk."

Justine took the clothes from Armon and changed. The sleep must have helped, she was thinking more clearly this morning. The panic and terror was in yesterday's memory. She was still afraid, but more able to control it. She thought on how much information Armon had given her through his periods of slipping into his past memories. Over the last 48 hours he gave her insight into his behavior. When she looked at him, now, she saw the eyes of a loving child in a man's body... a boy who'd lived a hellish childhood. A childhood so confused and twisted, his mind could not help but react abnormally. He had no gauge for normalcy. No sense of morality. His mother had been a child, when he was born. A weak child, hardly able to care for herself. So weak that she leaned on him to keep her going. She herself had been abused and in turn, abused her son, if not physically... emotionally. Her problems were multiplied upon him. Justine could not help feeling sorry for him. But she was feeling equally sorry for herself. She had to find a way out of this. She'd walked away from her last unsuccessful attempt. She couldn't count on being so lucky in the future.

Armon took her hand and led her down the path outside the cabin. He talked about things that had happened in the past, between him and his mother, expecting Justine to remember them. When he began to talk about the silver haircombs, he'd bought her, Justine's brain jumped to the alert.

100

"... I worked every little dirt job I could find to buy you those combs. You always wore them. It's too bad they got lost."

"But, Armon, I found them."

"You did. Where are they?"

"Back at the estate. Could we go and get them?"

"No... Montgomery..."

"But he's in jail. He won't be there. No one will be there."

Armon studied the ground and kicked some leaves. Then, slowly, he pulled Justine into his arms. "You really want them?"

"Of course, Armon. They were a gift from you. A very special gift. They are precious to me."

Armon held his face close to Justine's. "Alright. If they mean that much to you.."

"They do, Armon. They do."

"We'll get them."

Armon pressed his lips to Justine's, with a lover's passion. Justine reminded herself that whatever happened, it wasn't her fault. Whatever this person did to her, meant nothing. He was the one with the problem. He had a sickness of the mind. She was not at fault. She hadn't caused his affliction. She wanted to live through this. She would be an actress in a play. He had already once possessed her body. It wasn't worth dying to defend some archaic code of chastity. He could have her body. She would keep her soul.

Monday morning found Blake asleep at a desk in the North Carolina Police Barracks. One of the troopers woke him and provided a cup of coffee. "Thanks. Is there anything new?"

"Had a call from a deputy in Pomona. The woman might have bought some gas at a country store out that way. I'll drive you over... after you clean up."

Blake noticed he was a bit of a mess. "Yeah. I guess I need a shave."

"There's some supplies back in the locker room."

Blake looked slightly more human after a shave, but he felt like hell. When they arrived at Mrs. Dehaven's store, the deputy was there waiting for them. He introduced himself and Mrs. Dehaven.

"First I thought the bill might be counterfeit. But I had the bank check it out. It's good money. Then I heard the report about the possible hostage, I came back and asked Mrs. Dehaven to describe the woman. She fits the description."

The deputy pulled the bill from his pocket. "Mrs. Dehaven says the same word was scrawled across the bathroom wall, when she went in to clean this morning." The deputy handed the bill to Blake.

Blake read the word, then, sighed in relief. Justine was definitely alive. "Cascade. It's her. This was our project code name. No one else would know it. She was here."

Blake turned to Mrs. Dehaven. "When was this?"

"Saturday."

"Saturday... they could be anywhere by now. Did you see who she was with?"

"Yes. A young dark haired man. Very handsome."

"What about the car?"

"It was an older car. A Ford I think... light green."

The trooper interjected. "A light green Ford came up on the computer this morning. A missing person."

"He probably stole the car. You better get on the line and advise, the car may contain our fugitive and his hostage. No one should attempt to apprehend."

The trooper went to his car and radioed dispatch. Blake turned back to Mrs. Dehaven. "The woman... how did she look. Was she hurt or bruised or anything?"

"She looked like she'd slept in her clothes. Her clothes were a might too fancy for the car. Now that I think about it, she looked kind of scared. But I couldn't see she was in any danger. The man waited for her in the car and when she got in, they looked real friendly."

Blake thanked Mrs. Dehaven and she went back inside the store.

The trooper had a message that Blake should call Mr. Harold Compson, right away. Blake used the pay phone near the road. "What is it Harold?"

"Emergency Operations got a call, Saturday night. They think it was Ms. Edwards. She gave the code CASCADE, but the line went dead before she could say anything else."

"Did they get a trace?"

"Yes. The number was 555-8097." Blake wrote down the number.

"It's a pay phone in a town called Skyler. And Blake... they said she sounded like she was in real trouble."

"Thanks, Harold. I'll check in later."

The deputy had gone and the trooper was waiting, in the car, for Blake. Blake rushed to the car, got in and instructed the trooper to drive to Skyler. He explained as they drove.

The trooper had a theory. "The guy probably spotted the road block on highway 43 and went cross country to Skyler. I can even pick the road he took."

The trooper was running sirens and lights and burning up the road. "This is the right road."

Blake's knuckles went white, clutching the seat, as the trooper swung the car off the main road, making a hard left. The patrol car was taking a beating on the twists and turns and hills and valleys. "Geez, this is a regular roller coaster ride."

"That's why it isn't traveled much. There's a better road about 6 miles back."

By the time the patrol car wound down out of the hills and into Skyler, Blake wished they'd taken the other road. The trooper stopped the car near the phone booth Justine had used. "This is the only pay phone in Skyler."

Blake got out and checked the number, then walked back to the car. "It's the right number. You check in with the local authority. I'm going to look around."

The trooper drove away and Blake walked all around the phone booth, in an ever widening circle until he found some change lying in the dirt. He picked it up, then increased the circumference of the circle. Finding two safety pins tied together, he walked in a line straight away from the booth to find heel impressions in the soft earth bank along the road. He continued off the road into the grown up area. Upon finding trampled grass and broken twigs coming from the road above, he formulated what had happened. He waited by the roadside for the trooper to return.

The trooper got out and joined Blake at the roadside. "Find something?"

"Yes. It looks like she got away from him... up there on the hill. She ran straight down the hill here, up the bank..." Blake indicated the heel marks. "... and to the phone. She was trying to get change from her purse, while she was running. Some of it dropped in the road. I don't see any other heel impressions, so he didn't follow her down the hill, probably came down in the car and caught up with her at the phone booth. There's no sign of a fight... no blood. She's probably still alive. You find out anything?"

"The sheriff says one of the out of town residents reported their car stolen some time Saturday night or Sunday morning. It's a little silver sport job. And, there was a break-in at the department store just north of here. Only things missing were some women's clothes."

"Sounds like them. Justine is a good agent. She'll keep leading us, if she can. I'm sure they've crossed into Virginia by now. Can you arrange to put me with the Virginia State Police?"

"Sure, I'll put the call in and drive you up to the state line."

As the two entered the car, a call was coming through. The officer picked up the microphone and acknowledged. They had found the missing person from the light green Ford... shot through the head. The car had also been located north of Skyler, pushed into a ditch.

Blake was tense. "That does it, then. We're on the right trail. They're driving the silver sport car. Add the 'do not apprehend' to the stolen vehicle report and get me to Virginia."

Blake stared out the window and thought to himself. "I'll find you Justine. You just keep pointing me in the right direction. You're a damn good agent. I have to remember to tell you that... when I see you."

Blake transferred to the Virginia trooper's car. They checked every gas station and rest stop between the North Carolina line and the town of Catsburg before nightfall, with nothing to be found.

"Even if he had a full tank of gas, he couldn't have gotten much further than this."

"Maybe he took another car?"

"Maybe. Where's the next gas?"

"Willow Creek."

"How far is it?"

"Fifteen miles."

"We'll check there. If we don't find anything. We'll call it a night."

Blake was depressed and overly tired. He couldn't think anymore... he didn't want to think anymore. Think about Justine, being alone with Armon Dupree was all he'd done, since morning.

The small station in Willow Creek was closed, but the trooper managed to locate the owner and asked about the woman and man. The owner was pretty sure of the car, but he didn't see the woman. The man had paid for the gas.

Blake rode back to the barracks with the trooper. Upon meeting with the commander, they sat down with a map of the state and plotted the direction Armon would take, if... as Montgomery had indicated... Armon was heading for the sea. They plotted a course to Richmond, Petersburg, Virginia Beach and Newport News. All efforts were to be concentrated in those areas. The next report of Cascade moved them northeast, toward Richmond.

Blake was traveling one step behind them. The theory about traveling to the sea was shot through, when the next Cascade report came, indicating a sharp departure to the north. Blake went over and over in his mind... Where was Armon going? Where was he taking Justine? Nora? That was it! Armon thought Justine was Nora. He would react to her as if she were Nora. Armon's diary clearly showed that, in his mind, Nora and Justine were one and the same. Justine could manipulate him, if she worked it right. Blake smiled a broad knowing smile, as he gazed down at the map. The others in the room did not see what he was seeing. After a moment, he let them in on his secret.

"Wilson Falls! They're going to Wilson Falls. I don't know how she did it, but she's maneuvered him into going back to the estate. Good girl Justine! We'll be waiting! Commander, advise your men between here and Wilson Falls, to keep their eyes and ears open, but not to move in on them."

Blake made a call to Harold Compson. "Harold... Blake. Pull everybody out of the Montgomery Estate... fast. Justine is bringing him in. Hold everybody back till they are sure Justine is clear. Don't let them tip Armon off... or she's as good as dead."

Justine played her part well. There was no doubt in her mind that Armon had forgotten all about Justine Price and now accepted her totally as Nora Dupree. When they pulled through the gates of the estate, Justine prayed to see some sign that the Bureau still had someone on the grounds. There was none. The house was dark and everything was quiet.

Armon stopped the car at the front of the house and helped Justine out. "We'll go to the cottage, get the hair combs and be on our way to Richmond."

Armon took Justine's hand and started for the cottage. Justine thought. The cottage was too small to maneuver in... No place to run... No place to get away. Her best chance was the main house.

"No, Armon. They're not in the cottage. They're here in the house."

"Oh."

Armon used his key to unlock the door and they entered the dark house. Justine reached for the light switch, but was stopped by Armon. "Better not turn on any lights. Don't want anyone to know we're here. Where are they?"

She had to get him as far from the door as possible. Thus, once she escaped his reach, she'd have a chance to put distance between them and... maybe... get out of the house.

"Montgomery's apartment."

"What are they doing there?"

"He... he took them from me."

"Here, stay close to me. I know my way in the dark." Armon pulled her close, keeping his arm tight around her waist.

Finding the curtains drawn when they arrived in the apartment, Armon switched on a table lamp. "Where are they?"

"I think I saw him put them in the night table, in the bedroom."

Armon took Justine by the wrist and towed her into the bedroom with him. He let her go and crossed to the table.

Quickly, Justine turned and fled the room. Armon had been alert to her movement toward the bedroom door and caught her by the hair, as she crossed through the living room. Justine struggled with him and they fell to the floor, between the sofa and the coffee table. The television lit up, as the remote control fell beneath them.

Someone had left a movie in the VCR. At first, Armon paid no attention, then his eyes became riveted to the screen. It was the video of Nora and Montgomery. Armon held her fast beneath him, as he watched the two bodies locked in passion. His face took on the expression of a hurt little boy.

"Why did you do it, Mother? We had another chance to be happy. Why did you betray me with him... again? You know I hate him. It's happening all over again."

Armon's eyes were crazed. "You're going to make me do it all over, again."

Armon yanked Justine to her feet, then struck her hard, with the back of his hand. She fell upon the couch. Frantically, her mind raced, trying to piece together what was happening. Her eyes widened in terror, as she realized what Armon meant. Montgomery had not killed Armon's mother. Armon had killed her... out of jealousy. She had played her part so well... there would be no convincing Armon that she wasn't Nora... not now. At other times in her life, Justine had feared death. But, at no time, as much as she did right now.

Armon jerked Justine back up from the couch and held her close. "Tell me mother, is he better at loving you than I am? Do you enjoy it more with him? Do you?"

Armon shook her to loosen a response from her lips. Justine could not answer. With a vengeance, he struck her again, knocking her over the coffee table. As Justine fell, she lay upon the floor between Armon and the television. It still actively depicted titillating scenes of boundless intimacy, between Nora and Montgomery. Armon became once more fixed on the screen. Though dazed and full of pain, Justine dragged herself to her feet and unsteadily made for the door.

The door sprang open in front of her and three men, with guns, rushed in. Justine was pushed aside and the bullets flew, as a teary eyed Armon, drew on the three men. Armon had no chance of survival, as the pellets of lead penetrated his chest.

Relief drained the tension from Justine's body and she found there was no strength left to keep her upright. Her body drifted backward toward the wall and she slid to the floor. Before the encroaching blackness completely enveloped her brain, she heard someone saying "... call for an ambulance."

Chapter 10

Blake was ordered back to Washington and was not able to see Justine. She was kept in the hospital for observation, released, then flown home. Blake waited anxiously in the lounge, as the plane discharged its passengers. There she was, bruised, but still a welcome sight. Blake had made up his mind he was going to commit himself to her. Tell her how he really felt. How, he knew now, he'd felt for a long time. He smiled and started toward her. His smile faded, and he stopped cold, as the man he'd seen at Justine's apartment gathered her into his arms. He watched another moment, then turned, and left the airport.

Justine hugged her brother tightly, glad to be alive. As they walked from the lounge, Justine was looking all around... for Blake.

"Expecting someone else, sis?"

Justine sighed. "I thought maybe... no. Nobody."

Justine was given a week recovery time and Steve stayed with her, waiting on her and coddling her, till she could stand no more. She returned to work the following Monday, arriving early. She traveled down the Bureau halls, smiling to herself, about how "business as usual" everything was. She still looked the same. Her heels still made the same sound as they clicked against the polished floors. But there was something different about her eyes. They were still the same color, but there was a greater sense of self expression in them now... a confidence and wisdom, that only came when one saw, first hand, how precious life was.

Her associates wore expressions that told her they knew what a prize she'd won. The infamous Preston Montgomery had fallen, but they seemed not to realize she wasn't the one to fell him. Armon had given Montgomery to the Bureau. Justine had given them Armon, but not without help. She hadn't done it alone. The Bureau had given her her life... Blake had given her her life. Justine knew that he was responsible for saving her.

Worried about how she'd handle seeing Blake, after what had happened between them, Justine's smile slipped away. She had thought something special had happened. It would appear that Blake did not. It was hard thinking of herself as just a one night stand. She'd never given any thought to Blake being that kind of person. She'd given herself up to him, which was something reserved for a special few. And now, she felt betrayed and foolish.

She wondered how many of the other agents on this case knew what happened between Blake and herself. Would it be this week's topic of water cooler gossip?

Mr. Compson met Justine in the hall. "Ms. Edwards." He shook her hand. "I want to commend you on a job... more than well done. You went all the way for this one, and sacrificed a lot. We've moved you up 2 levels. You deserve it... and more."

"Mr. Compson, I didn't do it alone. I almost didn't do it at all."

"But the important thing is... you did. This case will stand out in your file for years to come. You should find yourself moving up rapidly, now. I know you've waited a long time for the recognition you deserved. You've waited longer than other... less qualified, and I was as well aware of that as you were. I was happy to see a big case come up that was custom made for you. You proved my faith in you... and the others... the ones that thought you were too inexperienced... they're kicking themselves. Speaking personally, I'm proud of you and I think you have a long career ahead."

Justine was embarrassed by all the flattery. "Thank you, Mr. Compson."

Steve appeared behind Mr. Compson. "Steve, what are you doing here? Is something wrong?"

Steve smiled broadly at Justine, as did Mr. Compson.

"What's going on?"

Mr. Compson took Steve's arm and pulled him up next to Justine. "I've hired your brother. If he's anything like his sister... Well, we're lucky to have both of you. Good luck Steve."

Mr. Compson patted Steve on the shoulder, then turned and started down the hall, toward the elevators.

Blake was coming up from records and stepped off the elevator to find Mr. Compson in front of him.

"Harold."

"Blake. Good job. I bet you're glad to finally close the file on that murder case. Screwy mess wasn't it. I never would have called that one. No wonder we had so much trouble with it. You did a hell of a job wrapping it up... figuring out what he was up to... where he was going."

"I'm glad to see Montgomery where he belongs and justice has been dealt to Nora Dupree's killer. But, don't compliment me for wrapping it up."

Blake motioned down the hall toward Justine, who was still standing with Steve. "She's the one that took the risks and brought it all down."

Blake continued to watch as Justine hugged Steve, they parted, and Justine went into her office.

"They make quite a pair don't they?"

Blake tried to be indifferent. "Quite."

"I only hope the fact that they're related won't cause a problem. I guess, if we stick to the policy about not putting relatives on the same case, we shouldn't run into any problems."

"Related?"

"Yes. Didn't you know? Steve's her brother."

"Brother?"

Surprise, then elation spread across Blake's face.

"What a jerk I am. Excuse me Harold. We'll talk later."

Just short of a run, Blake rushed down the corridor and into Justine's office. Justine was surprised at his bursting in.

"Oh. Good Morning, Mr. Hampton."

Blake didn't answer and closed the door. Justine was at a loss for what to expect from Blake. Was he here to try to shoot her down again? He'd made no effort to see her, since her return. Was he disturbed by what had happened between them? Maybe he felt awkward. Justine knew she did. Blake now stood less than a foot away, staring at her with a strange smile on his face.

"I was wrong about you, Ms. Edwards. You were ready for this assignment. You're a hell of a good agent. I'm just really sorry, we won't be able to work together any more. We'd have made a good team."

What was he saying. Was he quitting? She'd been promoted. Maybe he'd been moved up, too... to another department... another district?

"Why won't we work together, again?"

"Bureau policy... relatives can't work together on a case."

Justine was confused and it showed in her face. Had Blake gone crazy? Had this case caused him to snap? What was he talking about?

"But... we're not related."

"Technically, not yet. But you are going to say yes, aren't you?"

"Yes?"

"Good. It's official then."

"What's official? You're not making any sense, Mr. Hampton."

"Can't have you cailing me Mr. Hampton for the rest of our lives. Call me Blake. I intend to call you Justine."

He had gone crazy. Justine stepped back and reached for the phone. Blake grabbed her and pulled her into his arms.

"What's the matter? Trying to back out on your 'yes'? Don't like the name Hampton? You can keep yours, if you like. I have no problem with that."

Justine smiled, half afraid to put into words what she was thinking. "Did you ask me to marry you?"

"Gee, for a crack investigative agent... you're a little slow. I asked you and you said yes. Or have you found someone else in the last 60 seconds?"

Justine's smile spread contagiously across her face. "No, there's no one else."

"I love you, Justine Edwards."

His kiss was filled with the passion and obsession of a man in love. Justine had no reason to doubt it was genuine and fell gladly under his kiss.

Against Her Will

by T.J. Fox

*Dedicated
to
Myself*

... As partial restitution for the vacation I never got to take.

Chapter 1

The chartered plane gleamed and glistened in the early morning sun. Though small, the airstrip was well maintained. The boarding terminal was not elaborate, but it served its purpose. With a pleasant smile, the guard at the gate checked passports as the passengers boarded. He read their names aloud and bid each one of them to have a good flight. The passengers appeared to be indifferent to each other, and unacquainted. None of them boarded together. The guard's voice and actions were almost machine like. His job had become so automatic and uneventful, it was likely the names and faces were just a blur in his mind.

The passengers boarded, quietly and the guard looked at his watch, then down the hall toward the entry doors. There was one passenger missing. He smiled as he caught sight of a young, dark haired woman pushing her way hastily through the doors. She'd obviously been shopping during her short stay in Mexico. She even wore the full skirt, peasant blouse and sandals, thought to be so indicative of Mexican dress. Her breath came hard as she handed the guard her diplomatic passport. The guard smiled broadly, as he accepted it.

"Mrs. Stephanie Cantrel. Your husband told us you might be late. We had orders to hold the plane for you, but it seems you made it right on time. Have a good flight."

Stephanie took back her passport and thanked the guard. Still breathing heavily, she plopped down in her window seat. The door closed, the "Seatbelt/No Smoking" sign went on, and the plane began its ascent on what was to become the greatest adventure of Stephanie's life.

The plane passed over the water then crossed the shore leading to the dense green jungles over Bacaba.

Stephanie had not wanted to make this trip. She and her husband, Michael, argued fervently about it. Michael had referred to this trip as their "last chance" to save their troubled marriage and his career. Stephanie and Michael had never been a loving couple. Their marriage was arranged for political and social reasons. Stephanie resisted the union, until it became her dying grandfather's last wish. Being young and idealistic, Stephanie had little patience for the bureaucratic and sometimes self-righteous behavior of her husband. Michael referred to her as impulsive and irresponsible... to quote him, "a royal pain" and a "spoiled brat". Stephanie wanted a divorce, but Michael felt a divorce would be political suicide for him. He was tireless in his ineffective efforts to mold Stephanie into his ideal of the "perfect diplomatic wife".

His appointment as Ambassador to Bacaba was a feather in his political cap. He insisted that Stephanie live in Bacaba, with him. It wouldn't look good for him if she remained in the States. Finally, with reservations, Stephanie agreed to make the move.

Lazily, Stephanie slipped off her shoes and pulled her legs up into the seat. She gazed out the window trying not to think about anything. The jungle below appeared to be a solid covering of green. It reminded Stephanie of the grassy hills on Grandpa Nelson's farm in Virginia. She'd loved her visits with her grandfather and missed him badly when he died. She did wish that he hadn't been so insistent about her marriage to Michael. By making her promise to marry Michael, her grandfather, as he lay dying, could not have known what suffering it would cause her. If he were still alive, he would not pressure her to stay with Michael, the way her father did.

Without warning, three men with guns leapt into the isle. The big blonde man went to the cockpit, while the other younger, dark haired men held the passengers at gunpoint. The older of the two dark men spoke with a lilting Spanish accent. He was very handsome, not too tall, and his face spoke proudly of his ancestors. "Everyone stay in your seats, stay calm, and no one will be hurt. My friend here will come and collect your passports. You will give him your passport, slowly and no tricks."

The younger of the two men collected the passports without incident and carried them back to the older man. He accepted the passports, then ordered all the men to the seats in the rear of the plane, and all the women to the front. There was protesting and grumbling, but Stephanie remained cool. Somehow, she sensed it was she they were after. The man dropped all the men's passports to the floor. He picked up the women's passports and called their names. "Nancy Wilson, move to the back of the plane... Eileen Mason, to the back of the plane..." The two women moved quickly to the rear of the plane, leaving only Stephanie. The man stood directly beside her.

"Stephanie Cantrel..." He noted she was not wearing her shoes. "...Where are your shoes?"

Stephanie motioned back toward her previous seat. The man gestured to the younger one to retrieve her shoes. He did so, and handed the sandals to Stephanie. "Put them on."

Stephanie did as she was told.

The first man waited impatiently, until she was done. "Now stand up."

Stephanie hesitated and the man yanked her from the seat. She tried frantically not to panic, or scream, or otherwise lose control.

The first man spoke to the younger one. "Tell Jack we're ready." The young man carried the message, then came back and held the gun, while the first man donned a parachute.

The young man did the same and took the place of the man in the cockpit.

The first man, again, spoke to Stephanie. "Have you ever parachuted, before?"

Stephanie's eyes widened. "No...please..I don't know how."

"No matter. Listen to me. When I get ready to jump out this door, you will put your arms around my neck and you will hold on, as if your life depended on it... because it does. If you hold on, you will be safe. If you let go, you will be dead. You understand?"

Stephanie was shocked and confused. The man shook her, speaking slowly and directly into her face. "Do you understand?"

Stephanie, again, swallowed hard, and fought back the frightened tears, pushing their way into her eyes. "Y... yes."

"Are we low enough, yet?" The first man spoke to the big blonde, who had been with the pilot.

"Almost. Stand back. I'm going to open the door." The big man spoke with an accent...maybe Australian. "We're almost to the jump point. Get ready."

The first man put his gun away and pulled Stephanie close to him. "Wrap your arms around my neck, hold on and don't look down."

He needn't worry. She had no intention of looking down.

The big man hit the first man on the back. "Go."

The first man moved into the open doorway and jumped, holding Stephanie tight against his body. Stephanie closed her eyes. The sensation of falling, without restraint, was almost too much to stand. She felt panic forcing its way into her consciousness. The man spoke softly into her ear. "Just hold on and stay calm, you'll be all right."

Stephanie was amazed at the silly thoughts going through her mind. She wasn't dressed for this sort of activity... What did one wear to a kidnapping?

A sudden jerking motion indicated the parachute had opened, although Stephanie did not open her eyes to see. They began to float and drift in the wind. Stephanie braved herself and opened her eyes, slowly. The parachute spread over them like a bed canopy. She looked down and saw the green of the jungle moving toward them, at a much faster pace than she had anticipated.

"You're going to be all right." He spoke in a whisper. "When we land, we might land in a tree. If we do, I'll let you down. Don't panic! If we land on open ground, try to stay relaxed and bend your knees, otherwise, you'll break your legs."

"What a wonderful thought..." Stephanie's mind raced. "Two broken legs in the middle of the jungle."

An opening appeared below them and the man removed his arms from Stephanie, to help guide the parachute into it. The ground met Stephanie's feet and then her back, as her weight pulled the man down on top of her. A strange feeling swept over her, like an unexpected wind. The rush from the jump poured adrenaline into her body. She felt warm all over. Another feeling of excitement crept inside her. It had been exciting... frightening... but exciting.

The man lingered a moment over her, catching the feelings plainly visible in Stephanie's face. He rose, removed the parachute and spoke to Stephanie as she lay on the ground. "Are you all right? Do you hurt anywhere?"

Stephanie breathed deeply and wet her lips. "No... I don't think so."

The man offered Stephanie his hand. "Try to stand up."

Stephanie found her knees weak, from the experience, and began to fall. The man caught her in his arms. "Here..." He guided her to a fallen tree, nearby. "...sit down for a few minutes."

Stephanie thought this man was being very nice... for a kidnapper.

The man removed a walkie talkie from his pack. "Jack... Anzo... do you read me? Over."

An Australian voice answered him. "Jack here, you've drifted a bit off target, from the extra weight. Stay where you are and I'll be there before dark. Over."

"All right. Have you heard from Anzo? Over."

"No, but I saw where he went down. I'll check it out... How's our package?.. .All safe and sound? Over."

"Yes. All in one piece. Over."

"And a lovely piece at that. I'll see you before dark. Out."

The man put the walkie talkie away, then turned to Stephanie. "We may as well get comfortable. It will be a good 3 hours before Jack gets here. You stay put. I'm going to have a look around."

Stephanie's eyes widened. He was going to leave her here, alone.

"Don't worry, I'm not going that far. You're safe enough."

Stephanie remained silent and watched as the man disappeared into the deep green. She though about running, but where would she run? She'd wind up lost forever, in this endless twist of vines and leaves. They were probably going to hold her for ransom of some sort. They'd keep her alive... at least for awhile.

Stephanie made herself more comfortable on the ground near the tree trunk and waited. It seemed hours passed as the heat and humidity tortured her body. Being from the Northeast, she was not used to high temperatures, especially this type of heat. A rustling and crackling moved toward her from the green. Stephanie prayed it was the man and not some wild animal. Imagine, praying to see someone who had just stolen her away from her life. The man reappeared at the edge of the clearing. "Come with me. I've found a stream. You can wash up and cool off."

Stephanie followed the man through the dense tangle that tore at her clothing, bare arms, and legs. The bugs were equally persistent in making her uncomfortable.

The man ahead of her seemed oblivious to her plight, forging onward toward the water. A large thorny bush seemed to reach out and grab at Stephanie's leg, causing a trickle of blood from her thigh down to her ankle.

Stephanie wanted to cry, but refused to give in to the impulse. She'd show this bully that she wasn't a baby. He couldn't make her cry. Stephanie's Arien star sign was rearing its horns.

The stream was quite large and flowed swiftly in parts. The man led her to a still pool between two sand bars. He turned to speak to her, seeming surprised at what he saw. He didn't speak for a moment. Instead, he stared at the mess she'd become, on their short trek. Blood streaked her legs, arms and one side of her face. One arm of her blouse was torn and her skirt was in tatters. "Why didn't you say something?"

He looked both disgusted and disturbed. Stephanie didn't speak. The man sighed. "I have a uniform in my pack, I'll go back and get it. You go ahead and clean up. Oh, and don't drink the water. I have water in the canteens."

The man left and Stephanie stared into the water. It was so hot and she was so uncomfortable. Finally, she stripped down to her camisole and panties and slid into the water. The water soothed her irritated skin and relaxed the tense muscles in her body. She washed all the blood from her face and neck, then dipped under the water in an attempt to remove the debris from her hair.

After what seemed another, inordinately long time, the man returned with his pack. He sat on the bank and began removing things from his bag. He pulled out a military uniform and some socks, then sat silently watching Stephanie. He pulled a comb from his pack and placed it with the uniform. Stephanie turned her back to him, and, when she turned 'round again, he was gone.

She seized the opportunity to change into the uniform. She was painfully combing her hair when he returned, carrying a large handful of leaves. He pushed the leaves toward her. "Here. Crush them up and rub the liquid on your skin. It will help keep the bugs away."

Stephanie eyed him warily, then took the leaves. After crushing them and releasing their juices onto her fingers, she applied the slippery extract to her exposed skin. The smell was not unpleasant, but strong. Stephanie went back to combing the burrs from her hair, having a particularly bad time with the back. The man grabbed her wrist and took the comb from her. To Stephanie's amazement, he proceeded to remove the last of the tangles from her hair. He put the comb back in his pack and announced they would return to the clearing.

Stephanie followed, but they moved at a much slower pace than the first time. As Stephanie watched the man, just a yard ahead of her, she tried to figure out what kind of person he really was. So far, in her mind, he was a mass of contradictions. He couldn't be a totally bad person. Stephanie found it difficult to build up a feeling of hate for him. It just wouldn't come.

Once back at the clearing, the man produced food from his pack and water from the canteen. He handed some to Stephanie. She ate the food and found she was very tired. Crumpling up her tattered skirt, she made a pillow then lay her head on it. Once her eyes closed, she was lost in a profound and dreamless sleep.

She woke to the sound of men's voices. The man called Jack and the man called Anzo had arrived. The young man seemed to be injured, although not seriously. Stephanie sat up, watched, and listened to the men. She heard the two arrivals call the man who brought her to earth, Amelio. The name suited him, a gentle name, for an unusual man. A name Stephanie would remember.

Amelio tended Anzo.

The fact that Stephanie was now awake, caught Jack's attention. He walked toward her and crouched down beside her. "How'd you get that skirt off of her, Amelio? I wish you'd have waited for me." Jack was being crude and his manner was frightening to Stephanie, though she tried not to show it.

"What did you do, throw her in a briar patch? She's all cut up.'" Jack put his hand to Stephanie's face. "A shame to mar that pretty face."

Amelio completely ignored Jack's remarks. "When will we start for Valdez, Jack?"

"I think we'll stay here tonight and get a fresh start in the morning."

"Do you think it safe? Won't they come looking?"

Jack continued to watch Stephanie, as he talked with Amelio. "They'll never find us in this jungle, and they know it. They'll just wait for a call."

Stephanie could see inside Jack, through his eyes. He could not be trusted. He possessed an animal's instinct for survival and his passions were loosely controlled, at best. The man's smile hid the teeth of a wolf. His face appeared handsome, but was only a mask, hiding a sinister monster. His eyes... It was all there... in his eyes.

Chapter 2

The three day journey through the jungle began with the sunrise. Amelio shook Stephanie gently to wake her and they started out right after breakfast. Jack pushed them hard all morning. Stephanie tried her best to keep up. Anzo brought up the rear and was obviously distressed at having to lag back with her. He was a zealous, attractive young man in his late teens. Full of the spirit of adventure. He would have preferred to be up front where the action was, instead of babysitting with Stephanie.

Finally, they stopped to rest and eat. Stephanie was entirely too tired to think about the food. She lay down on the ground in exhaustion. The heat and the humidity made her feel as if she were dragging along a weight. Her clothes were heavy with moisture and breathing was difficult. The air hung thick with the smell of rotting undergrowth, occasionally mixed with a whiff of something sweet, like flowers or fruit. Amelio offered her a drink from the canteen and she took it, wearily. She handed it back to him.

"We are following not too far from the river. You rest awhile, then I'll take you to the water and you can cool off. I imagine this heat is a bit intense for someone not a native."

Stephanie nodded.

"Amelio..." Jack was calling from up ahead. "... come up here."

Amelio vanished up the trail leaving Anzo behind, again. Stephanie leaned back against a tree and looked up into the green canopy. There were many birds chattering away. It seemed they were happy to be alive today. Stephanie's eyes dropped to the green of the tree just behind Anzo. Her eyes had perceived a small movement above Anzo's head. She couldn't see exactly what it was, at first. But then, she saw the head of a snake poised above Anzo, ready to strike. Instinctively, Stephanie lunged for Anzo, knocking him out of the way. Not for a second did she think about letting the snake strike him.

Before her trip here, she had read a book on snakes native to the area. Hating snakes as she did, she wanted to know what to expect. She knew that most of them were very poisonous. Here, in the jungle, a snake bite could be more deadly than ever. Despite their current relationship, Stephanie couldn't justify letting the boy die.

The two rolled several times, before Anzo pushed her away, angrily. "What the hell are you doing!" Jack and Amelio stood a few feet away.

Jack spoke. "She's saving your tail, my friend."

Jack raised his pistol and shot the snake in the head. Instead of being grateful, Anzo was annoyed at being made to look foolish. He stormed away in a huff.

"Anzo..." Amelio tried to call him back.

"You better go after the kid, Amelio. I'll take her to the river."

Jack held his gaze tightly on Stephanie, as he spoke. Amelio hesitated.

"Go on. Go after the kid, before he gets into any more trouble."

Amelio trotted off, after Anzo.

"Well, come on, hero. Let's get cooled off."

Fearfully, Stephanie followed the man. He cleared a small space at the river's edge so they might gain access. Jack threw his machete past Stephanie and it stuck in a tree. He pulled off his gear, dropped his hat and shirt over it, then sat to remove his boots. Stephanie just stood by, watching.

"Go ahead, get your shoes off. Get wet."

Reluctantly, Stephanie sat and took off her shoes and socks. Jack had already waded out into the stream. He stood waist high in the water, throwing it onto his hairy chest. Stephanie couldn't help thinking how ape-like he was. She walked to the edge and waded ankle deep into the water.

"Come on, get yourself wet. Once we start moving again, we won't stop till nightfall. You won't get another chance till then."

Stephanie didn't move any further into the water. She bent down and lifted some water to her face and neck. Silently, Jack moved ever closer to her, much as the snake had crept up on Anzo. Until, without warning, he reached out, pulling her into the water.

"Modesty must go my dear. Here, I'll help you with your shirt."

Jack was very strong and, it seemed, very determined. He pushed Stephanie beneath the water and held her there, while he finished unbuttoning her shirt with his other hand. As he pulled her to the surface, he jerked the shirt from her arms and flung it to shore. She still wore her shiny pink camisole and it clung tightly to her breasts as she gasped for air.

Jack may have intended further plans for Stephanie, but they were put on hold, as Amelio's voice resounded from the shore. "Jack..."

"Amelio... Did you find Anzo?"

"Yes, I found him. What's going on?"

"Nothing. Just getting cooled off. Right Stephie?" Jack held Stephanie's wrist below the water surface. He twisted it in a threatening manner. Stephanie nodded her affirmation and Jack let her go. She waded back to shore and redressed, still coughing slightly for having swallowed some water.

Jack went on about his business, as if nothing had happened. He certainly was a cool customer. Nothing seemed to frighten or disturb him.

Amelio cooled himself, then led Stephanie back to where they had stopped. "You want something to eat now? Once we get moving again we won't stop for a long time."

Stephanie shook her head, no.

Amelio stood above Stephanie as she sat on the ground. "Listen, I appreciate what you did for Anzo, even if he does not. He is just a boy. It hurt his pride. He'll get over it."

Stephanie made no response and Amelio moved away.

Jack and Anzo took the lead this time, with Amelio behind Stephanie. By nightfall, they had reached a joyful little waterfall. Jack indicated they should stop there for the night. Stephanie didn't sleep well. Though exhausted, she was nervous and afraid of falling asleep. Every little jungle noise, no matter how minor, drew her attention and kept her away from a sound sleep. Come morning she was not rested.

Amelio and Anzo were arguing about something in Spanish, when Stephanie woke. It seemed Amelio finally won the argument. Amelio collected his gear and came to Stephanie.

"Jack and I will be gone all day. We must go on ahead. Anzo will stay here with you."

Stephanie looked up at Amelio, with the frightened eyes of a child. It seemed each passing hour in this hostile environment brought her one step closer to breaking down into tears. A softness moved over Amelio's face. He knelt beside her and whispered to her. "Everything is going to be all right. You are going to be all right. Trust me." His eyes showed genuine concern and Stephanie felt a blind trust, in this man she hardly knew.

Amelio stood up, said something to Anzo in Spanish, then moved off up the trail.

Soon after Amelio left, Anzo vanished. Momentarily, Stephanie thought they had all gone off and left her to die, but that thought faded. They needed her alive to ensure whatever ransom they were asking. They'd be back. She cooled herself in the water and, since she would not be traveling for some time, she changed back into her skirt. Though tattered, it was cooler than the military uniform. She sat beside the waterfall for hours, floating little leaf boats into the water.

Anzo returned around noon day and offered Stephanie some food. She was hungry and accepted it.

Later in the day, near dark, Jack returned, without Amelio.

"Where is Amelio?" Anzo questioned Jack.

"He is waiting for a message from the general. He'll be here soon enough."

Anzo was not pleased to be again left out. Stephanie was uneasy. She felt Amelio was the only thing that stood between her and this man-animal that watched her with hungry eyes. Jack had brought back some "real food" to cook for dinner. He handed it to Anzo and told him to build the fire. Grudgingly, Anzo did as he was told.

Jack removed his gear and sat next to Stephanie. "I like the skirt much better. I'm glad you changed... You don't talk much. That's good. Some of the women I've taken have been such trouble, always screaming and crying, trying to get away. You're smart, you know to keep your mouth shut and do as you're told. That's the only way you'll survive this."

Jack placed his hands on her shoulders and massaged them. "I bet you're really stiff from all this sleeping on the ground. Here... I'll rub your neck."

Stephanie thought it best not to offer any resistance. As much as she didn't want to admit it, what he was doing felt good. She was stiff.

Anzo began to prepare the meal and was doing a clumsy job of it.

"Anzo, not like that. Haven't you ever cooked anything before?" Jack was annoyed. "Here. Take over for me and I'll cook it."

Anzo looked at Jack in puzzlement.

"Come on kid. Get over here."

Anzo came.

"Put your hands right here and work it, you know like you're working a dough, only gently."

Anzo was awkward at first, but his technique improved as Jack kept talking to him as he prepared the meal. "Gentle Anzo... You must handle them gently, sometimes... Wear them down, so they're less resistant. Feel how soft her skin is, Anzo? Have you ever had a woman before, Anzo? Do you know how they feel... all over? How they smell? Put your face down to her neck Anzo. You see, even with this heat, she still smells like a woman... not a man."

Stephanie wasn't at all sure just what Jack was up to, but she was frightened. Maybe that's what he wanted... to frighten her.

"Now move your hands out to her shoulders and down her arms. Keep rubbing up and down. Feel the tension disappear under your hands."

Jack's eyes seethed with delight as he watched Anzo. Stephanie could feel Anzo's breathing change. He pushed her blouse down over her shoulders, baring them and much of her back. She could no longer control her trembling. Adrenaline pumped again. The memory of riding a roller coaster flew through Stephanie's mind like a cold winter wind. She was beyond word or action. She sat petrified, as this boy pressed his hands on her while Jack watched ecstatically.

"Go for it Anzo." Jack's voice urged the boy on. "Take her. She's ready."

Anzo pushed Stephanie to the ground and placed his convulsive body over hers. Stephanie steeled her eyes on Jack and blocked out what was happening with Anzo.

Finding her voice, she shouted at Jack. "Coward!" She shouted at Jack. "Having a boy do your dirty work. What's the matter... you not capable?" Stephanie could hardly believe she was saying these things.

Jack flew into a rage. His face filled with a cruelty she hoped never to see again in her life. He jerked Anzo to his feet and pushed him aside. Stephanie questioned herself now. Why had she said that? Why had she provoked him?

Jack stood over her menacingly, then... he smiled, and walked back to the fire. Stephanie sat up and smoothed back her hair, still very tense and wondering what was to come.

Jack chuckled, went back to the meal and spoke to Stephanie across the fire. "You're good honey. You almost made me do it. You almost made me do something stupid. No. It's not time for you and me. Not time... yet. But there will be a time. You'll just have to wonder about it. You'll never know when it will be... When you least expect it, I think. Yes, you'll be good and surprised when it happens." Jack waved Anzo away. "Go cool off Anzo. Take a walk."

Anzo was confused and frustrated, but he didn't feel confident enough to go up against this man.

Jack fixed a plate of food for Stephanie and brought it to her. "By the time it finally happens, Stephie, you'll be begging me to do it and get it over with. You'll beg me." He ran his massive hand across her shoulder and handed her the plate.

Stephanie realized, now, that Jack was adept at psychological games. He was trying to control her through her own fear. She had to keep this ever forefront in her mind. She would have to stay calm at all times or he would win the game he played with her mind. He would be like the "Jack-in-the-box". She would never know when he would pop up with something.

For the first time, Stephanie really analyzed her situation. Jack was the number one threat. He might kill her. Anzo was basically indifferent to her, unless provoked. Only Jack could make him a threat to her. Amelio was her ticket to safety, but she wasn't sure he could stand against Jack. Amelio had scruples and Jack did not. The only rules Jack played by were his own. She had to tie herself to Amelio and hope for the best.

Anzo returned to camp and sat on the far side of the fire, across from Stephanie. He would look at her every once in a while, in a guilty manner. Jack lay, sprawled out, not far from Stephanie, half asleep. Stephanie sat huddled, trying to hold herself together.

Amelio returned about an hour after dinner. Intense fear was clearly visible on Stephanie's face and Amelio perceived it. He looked first at Jack, who hadn't moved a muscle, then at Anzo. Guilt dripped from Anzo's face in every bead of perspiration. "Anzo, what happened?"

Anzo hesitated and looked away. "Nothing!"

"Anzo..."

"Nothing happened! Ask Jack!"

Amelio kicked Jack's boot and Jack stirred lazily.

"What's up, Amelio? Hear from the general?"

"What is going on here? What has happened?"

"Well, I killed about 200 mosquitoes, we had some pretty good grub and I was just catching some beauty sleep. Sound exciting?"

"I don't think I need to remind you that we need her in good condition."

Jack peered at Amelio from under his hat. "My job was to help you get her off the plane and take all of you to Valdez. There were no 'health guarantees' in my contract. I'll do my job. I'll get all of you to Valdez, collect my money and be gone. This is your cause... not mine."

Amelio was not going to argue. He turned away from Jack and towards Stephanie. Leaning over, he grabbed her by the arm and pulled her to her feet. "Come with me."

He led her away from the fire to a small crescent of rocks, not far from the others. He dropped his gear and started to bed down for the night, leaving Stephanie standing, watching. After a moment, he lay down and patted the ground on the far side of him. "You better sleep here with me, tonight."

The words came strictly as an order, with no ulterior intent. Stephanie wasn't going to protest. She knew it was the safest place for her, under the current circumstances.

Chapter 3

Next morning, Stephanie changed back into her traveling clothes. They passed over some very rocky terrain that day. Several times Stephanie lost her footing and fell, causing many bruises over her tired body. Amelio kept her close to him at all times throughout the day, training a watchful eye on both Jack and Anzo. He made a number of attempts to pry the previous evenings events from Anzo, but Anzo wasn't talking. He knew it was pointless to ask Jack.

"Jack..." Jack turned to listen to Amelio. "We're running behind schedule. We're not going to make it by tonight."

"Well, damn, man. You gotta quit stopping every time the lady falls down!"

"I think you and Anzo should go on ahead. Make sure there are no problems and send word that we'll be a little late."

Jack looked thoughtfully at Amelio. Then, he turned his eyes to Stephanie and smiled. He kept his eyes on her. "Yeah, I guess that might not be a bad idea, but aren't you worried she might kill you in your sleep?"

"She knows she'd be lost out here in the jungle, without me. I'm not worried."

Anzo started to object. Jack interrupted him. "Come on kid. Let's go. We can sleep in a bed tonight." Jack put his arm around Anzo's shoulder. "Maybe we can get you a woman tonight, kid. Come on."

Stephanie slid down the rocks, to a seated position. Every muscle in her body ached. With Jack gone, Stephanie felt a modicum of relief. Silent tears trickled down her cheeks, but she wasn't aware she was crying. Amelio built a fire and fixed them some food. Stephanie ate only a few bites. Her stomach felt queasy, and her head hurt.

"We will be in Valdez tomorrow. You will be more comfortable there. Your husband has been contacted and is waiting instructions. You won't have to wait too much longer... maybe a week." There was a long pause. "You don't say much."

Stephanie sighed. "I might say the wrong thing."

"Is that what happened with Anzo and Jack?"

"No."

"I want to know what happened."

"Why?"

"I'm responsible for your safety and it is important that I know what is going on in those two mens' heads."

"I think you already know what's going on in Jack's head. As for my safety... you may not be able to guarantee it. Not with Jack around."

"And why is that?"

Stephanie wondered if this man were really all that blind. "Jack is going to rape me." Stephanie's words were calm and direct.

Amelio appeared shocked by her candor. "What makes you think that?"

Stephanie was becoming annoyed with the third degree. Her head hurt and she was in no mood for conversation. "He told me."

"And Anzo?"

"Jack can manipulate him. As you said, he is just a boy. He is easily provoked."

136

"Why don't we quit dancing around this and you tell me just what happened."

Stephanie leaned her head back against the rock. "Jack provoked Anzo into attacking me, because Jack wasn't ready to do it himself... I guess he wanted to watch..." Stephanie looked for reaction in Amelio's face.

"... I called Jack a coward for having Anzo do his work... Jack flew into a rage... He pulled Anzo off of me... and stopped just short of doing the job himself."

Stephanie's brave facade slipped a bit, and she looked away. Putting into words, just what happened, made it a reality and not a distant dream. Stephanie's control was weakening.

"This does present me with a problem."

"More than you think, I'm afraid."

"What do you mean?"

Stephanie spoke plainly. "You said my husband has been contacted?"

"Yes."

"He will most likely not pay the ransom."

"Why would he not pay, knowing that might mean your death?"

"Because my husband does not love me, nor I him. We have a marriage of convenience. I've asked him for a divorce, but he refuses... because of his career. This is his perfect opportunity to be rid of me, without having it reflect badly on him. You've made it very convenient for him. It will probably even help his career if I am killed... all the sympathy."

"This cannot be true. He must have some feeling for you."

"Possibly some disappointment, resentment, maybe contempt. He wanted my family's good name and social standing to further his career. I only married him at my grandfather's insistence. Michael is a selfish, egotistical, hypocrite." Stephanie's state of agitation was increasing.

Amelio paced back and forth, before speaking further. "Is there anyone else who would pay the ransom?"

"My father would, if someone went directly to him and he was sure it was not a ruse."

"Is there a way to convince your father, that you are really a captive."

"Yes, if I can write him a note. He will believe."

Amelio looked worried. He paced the campsite a few time, then went off into the jungle. While he was away, Stephanie rummaged through his pack for first aid items. Then she stripped down to her camisole and panties in order to tend her many bites, scratches and bruises. The alcohol from the pack burned the scratches, but Stephanie was all too well aware how a small cut could become infected, under these environmental conditions. The largest cut on her thigh, already showed signs of infection. She was busy trying to clean the cut when Amelio returned.

Amelio watched her from a distance, before he spoke. "That doesn't look good. I have something in my bag for it."

Amelio retrieved a packet from his bag. He moved close to Stephanie and ripped open the packet. He looked Stephanie squarely in the face. "This is going to hurt like hell. Scream if you want to."

Stephanie chose not to watch, as he sprinkled the powder over the cut. He had been right, it hurt like hell and there was no way to get away from it. It burned like a flame, since that was exactly what it was doing. It burned the infection and the cut, till Stephanie thought she would pass out. Slowly, the pain subsided to a dull agony.

Amelio crumpled the packet and tossed it into the fire. "I find you very strange, Mrs. Cantrel."

"Forgive me, if I say the same."

"No. I don't mean strange in that sense. I mean, you have been through much hardship these few days. Yet you have complained very little."

"Would complaining have done me any good?"

"No. I expect we would have found it very irritating."

"You see. I would have made myself and everyone else more irritable. It might have been so bad, that you could have decided to shoot me and put everyone out of their misery."

Amelio smiled at her backhanded levity, as he placed a bandage over the cut. "Here. Let me look at you and make sure you haven't missed anything. Let me see your back."

There was a large bruise just over her shoulder blade. "That must have happened, when I fell on you, when we landed. Does it hurt much?"

"To tell you the truth, I hurt everywhere. It's all just kinda one big hurt."

Amelio went back to his bag and produced some small white pills. "Are you allergic to any medicines?"

"No."

"Then take this." Amelio handed her a pill from the vial. "What is it?"

"A pain killer. Take it. You'll be able to sleep better." Amelio handed her the canteen and she downed the pill.

"I'll get some more leaves to ward off the bugs. I'll be right back."

Amelio brought the leaves and helped Stephanie apply the pungent juice over her skin. "Sleep as you are. Give your clothes a chance to dry out some... and your body a chance to breath. I would have suggested it before, but I sensed Jack might be a problem."

Amelio was very close to Stephanie. Stephanie felt an almost tangible ripple flow between them. Amelio must have felt it as well, because he moved away quickly. Stephanie was all too well aware of her attraction to Amelio. There was a chemistry between them... an electricity. Had they met under other circumstances, Stephanie knew they'd have been lovers. As it was, she was having much difficulty thinking of him as her captor and not a close, caring friend. He must have a very good reason for participating in her kidnapping. Judging from the way his eyes shone when he spoke about Bacaba and the current revolution, she suspected his participation revolved around his patriotism. He was a highly intelligent, educated man, and there was nothing ruthless or cruel about him. Stephanie could not see him as a criminal... and certainly not as a cold blooded killer.

Anzo was different, but equally as benign in his heart. He was merely caught up in the "romance" of a cause. He was too young and too impulsive, to fully understand what he was doing. Stephanie could imagine his mother, worrying over her impetuous, rebellious son. He was still an innocent, subject to the influences of more dominant persons.

Jack was a totally different breed... a mercenary... a gun for hire. He was obviously a professional. He indicated he'd done this before. Stephanie wondered how many women had fallen under his merciless hands. How many of them didn't have an Amelio to keep them from his abuse? How many of them never survived their abduction? Stephanie's stomach churned with fear, as she thought on what might happen to her... left in Jack's hands.

Amelio interrupted Stephanie's thoughts. "Tell me more about your husband. Is he going to be a good ambassador to my country?"

"Oh, yes. One thing about Michael, he does his job very well."

"Surely, you could have divorced him, despite his protest?"

"Maybe. But, I guess I feel sorry for him. His career is everything in his life. If he loses that, he will have nothing. Besides, there is no one else for me right now. If there were..."

"I still have trouble believing he would allow you to be killed."

"Believe me. I know how he thinks. If it would further his career, he would allow it."

"You better go to sleep. I want to start early in the morning."

They rose with the sun, but Amelio kept the pace slow and allowed Stephanie many stops for rest. It was almost, as if he never wanted to arrive in Valdez. Stephanie had expected to see a city when they reached their destination. Instead, Valdez turned out to be a tiny village. They stopped at a small house, near the edge of the village. It was more or less a mud hut, with a thatched roof. It was sparsely furnished and dark.

Jack and Anzo sat at the table playing cards. Jack threw his cards on the table. "Well it took you long enough. My money isn't here and there has been no response from her husband. What the hell is going on?"

"There has been a change in plans. We are going to take a ransom note to her father, instead of her husband."

"Ha! Her husband doesn't want her back, does he? It's not the first time I've run into this. Are you sure her old man will pay?"

"Yes. But someone has to deliver the ransom note directly to her father. Otherwise, he will think it a scam."

"Well, then I'm the man for that job. This time I'll make sure I get my money. Give the lady some paper so she can write her daddy a note."

Anzo produced a pad of paper and a pencil. Stephanie sat at the table and wrote the note. "He will know it is me, by what I have written. He will give you what you ask for."

"I'll leave first thing in the morning." Jack took the note, folded it and stuffed it into his pocket.

He reached across the table and grabbed the front of Stephanie's shirt. "You had better be right this time little lady, or I'll come back and get my payment in another way."

Amelio grabbed Jack's arm. "Let her go."

"Sure mate, but I'm serious. Someone is going to finish paying me for this job."

"You'll get your money. One way or another, you'll get what you deserve."

"I better."

Jack left the next morning, before first light. Anzo was still asleep, but Amelio stood in the door, watching the sunrise. Stephanie woke feeling very thirsty. Her head pounded, she felt weak and clammy. Shakily, she sipped water from the canteen, then passed out cold on the floor. Amelio heard her fall, went to her, and lifted her back to the bed. He felt her face, covered her with a blanket, then woke Anzo.

"Anzo, you must go to the next village and bring back the doctor. She has the fever."

"But she only drank water from the canteen..."

"I think Jack did it. When I left you that day... after the snake... Jack had her in the water. I think he was holding her under. She was coughing like she had swallowed water."

Anzo was struck with remorse. "Amelio... I never meant to hurt her... I couldn't control myself... I... She saved my life."

"Never mind that now, Anzo. It's 15 miles or better to the next village, you better get started."

Anzo left hurriedly. He felt guilty about his past transgression and felt now he was being punished. If she died, he would carry the guilt forever.

Amelio set about removing Stephanie's clothes and bathing her in cool water. He knew the basics of caring for the fever, but he had no medicine. He never thought he would need it. He had made sure of their drinking water.

She must have been ill for some time, to have the fever this bad. She never once complained or indicated she was ill. In Amelio's eyes, she was a very courageous and brave hearted woman. The type of person you could depend on and take at their word. Amelio had not been delighted with the general's decision to do this deed. He wished now he had refused to carry it through. This woman was a person, with feelings... not an enemy.

It rained all afternoon, something that was not good for the fever. Amelio sat with her, bathing her face and listening to her talk in her sleep. Despite her brave front... she was very much afraid for her life. Jack had become a nightmare to her. Amelio was both surprised and pleased to find he had taken a place of affection in her heart. As she mumbled his name, it became all too clear to him, that he had formed an affectionate attachment for her as well. This caused a great deal of confusion for Amelio. How could this have happened? Why had it happened? What would come of it?

Luckily, the doctor in the next village owned a horse and wagon. He arrived the next morning. Upon examining Stephanie, he found her to be gravely ill. He gave her the medicine, but was not at all sure she would survive. "She's been ill for several days. Why did you wait so long?"

"I had no idea she was ill. She never said anything."

"Who is this woman?" The doctor asked in a suspicious manner.

"She is my wife."

"And you are?"

Amelio thought before he answered. There was no reason to hide his identity from this man. "Amelio Cadeez."

"General Cadeez's son?"

"Yes."

"You have no need to worry. I am a loyal follower of the cause. I will not speak of you to anyone. But she is very ill. If the fever does not break by nightfall, I fear she will be lost. Unfortunately, I cannot stay. The militia made a raid in Abdoro. I must go there to help the injured. Keep working on the fever. You must bring it down. If she makes it through the night, she has a good chance. I wish you luck. Goodbye."

"Good bye doctor, and thank you for coming."

Anzo became very distressed. "She's going to die and it will be may fault. If I hadn't acted like a baby and you hadn't come after me, he wouldn't have been alone with her. It's my fault."

"Anzo, stop it." Amelio took Anzo by the shoulders. "It was not your fault. If there is anyone to blame it is Jack. He is to blame for this, not you. He did the deed. And, she is not going to die. I won't allow it and neither will you. We have to believe, she *will* live, and she will live. She is a brave woman. You notice how she never cried even when she was hurt. She is strong in her heart. She will make it... between the three of us... she will live."

One of them tended her every moment of the day. The fever hadn't budged. Stephanie lay pale and deathly quiet save for an occasional low moan. The sun moved lower and lower in the sky, until only a pink cloud remembered it's light. Amelio stood despairingly, in the doorway. Suddenly he was struck with a memory from his childhood.

"Anzo..." He shouted for the boy. "... build a fire and heat some rocks in it, right away."

Anzo stared at Amelio, as if he'd gone mad.

"Anzo, remember when you were about 7 or 8, when the fever was bad and people were dying? Remember old mama Cezaro? Her son Tonio was so ill and his fever would not stop. Remember... they heated rocks in the fire, put them in a tent made from blankets. They threw water on the rocks and made steam, took Tonio inside till he was very very warm, then put him in the river. It broke the fever!"

"Yeah, I remember. It almost killed him. He was never quite right after that."

"Anzo... if we don't try it... she's going to die anyway. I think we have to take the risk."

"All right."

Anzo made everything ready. Amelio wrapped Stephanie tightly in a blanket and carried her into the steam tent. He stayed inside with her, until the blanket and he were thoroughly soaked. Then, quickly, he carried her to the stream and dunked her body in the water. Her body reacted to the shock, convulsively. He held her there till he could feel the cold, deep in his own bones. Weakened himself by the process, he carried her back to the house, wrapped her in a dry blanket and checked her temperature. It had dropped.

"It's down, Anzo... 2 degrees! I think we did it!"

The two men continued to sit with Stephanie over the course of the night and into the next morning. Anzo fell asleep at the table. Amelio fell asleep with his head resting near Stephanie on the bed, as to feel her should she wake. He was in an exhausted sleep, at first unaware of her waking.

Stephanie woke to find him there. She was vaguely aware of how sick she had been and how he had cared for her. Softly, she touched her hand to his head and his eyes opened in excitement.

"You are alive!"

"Thanks to you it seems." Stephanie's voice was weak.

"I guess I owed it to you. Are you hungry?"

"Yes, but I'm too tired. I think I'll go back to sleep."

"Yes. You sleep. When you wake, I'll have something for you to eat."

It was days before Stephanie gained enough strength to venture out of bed. She stood outside the house in the sunshine, not even minding how hot it was. She was glad to be able to feel the sun on her face. Amelio approached from the road into the village.

"I'm glad to see you up. I brought you something. Come inside." Amelio dropped a bundle onto the table and opened it, slowly, to reveal a lovely skirt and blouse, much like the ones she wore on the plane.

"They are from the women here in the village. They think you are my wife. They are glad you are well, and want you to feel good with some new clothes."

Amelio left the house to allow Stephanie to change. She dressed and joined him outside. Stephanie was awkwardly embarrassed, but she had to say it. "It seems rather silly for you to leave, when I change. I mean, you took care of me when I was sick... I remember... Well, you know."

Amelio smiled at the blush in her cheeks. "You are a very beautiful woman... on the inside as well as the outside. Your husband is a fool. Given a chance, you could make anyone a good wife."

Stephanie went sullen. "Have you heard from Jack?"

Amelio looked away. "Yes, he is on his way back. There will be an even exchange, you for the money... Kazra Plaza next week, in San Sabo."

"I see. Well, I knew daddy would come through."

"It seems he loves you very much."

"In his own way, he loves me. But he doesn't place much worth on my happiness. He keeps the pressure on me to stay married to Michael."

Stephanie broke from her somber tone. "So... how much did you get?"

Amelio gave her a sidelong glance and moved a few feet away. "If it were up to me... I would just let you go. The money is needed for medicine and ammunition. We are so close to achieving our takeover... It could come any day. If that were to happen, there would be no need for this. I could just let you go. Every day now, I pray for it to happen. I wish we'd never gone through with this. I was against it...

but this is a war and we cannot always follow our hearts. Sometimes, we must follow orders." Amelio was thoughtful. "There is so much inequity in this country. It must change and revolution is the only way."

"You believe very strongly in your cause, don't you?"

"Yes, I do. Many of us do."

"Why would you get mixed up with someone like Jack?"

"Jack, though I do not like him, has the expertise in these things. We need that expertise. It is unfortunate that this world is not an idyllic place. There is always compromise. We try to minimize it, as much as possible. Some people will die for our cause. Some people will suffer for it... but in the end, all the people who have suffered, for so long, will be allowed to live a better life."

Amelio sighed loudly, as he looked out over the jungle. "But how could you possibly understand such things. You are an American. You have never suffered oppression, starvation and poverty."

"Amelio, I may not ever have experienced those things, but I do know they exist... and they shouldn't. I understand your devotion to your cause. I would, however, question how much you are willing to compromise. Won't there come a point when the revolutionaries become the same as those now in power. Is there a line drawn, you won't cross?"

Amelio turned to her in a defensive manner. "I would never knowingly allow an innocent to be harmed for my personal benefit. I would never blame my wrong doing on another. And, I would not place my life above another's."

Stephanie felt he had put her in her place and remained quiet. Amelio disappeared for the rest of the day.

Chapter 4

Two nights passed. Stephanie lay sleeping, suddenly to be awakened by a hand pressed over her mouth. Her eyes widened with fear, as she saw it was Jack.

"Be quiet and listen. You're father has paid me to get you out of here."

Stephanie was disbelieving.

"Here, look." Jack produced a small gold locket that once belonged to Stephanie's grandmother. As he did, a slip of paper fell from his pocket, unseen.

"He said you would know this." Jack dangled the locket in front of her eyes.

Stephanie nodded and Jack removed his hand from her mouth. Stephanie dressed and followed Jack into the night, with great misgivings.

When Amelio woke, he immediately saw that Stephanie was missing. He called to her, but she did not answer. He spied the small piece of paper from Jack's pocket on the floor near Stephanie's bed. It was a baggage ticket from an American airline.

"Jack..."

Amelio woke Anzo. "Jack came back, and he has taken Mrs. Cantrel. Quickly, they can't have been gone long."

The men packed hurriedly and Amelio set the course. "This way, he'd want to get as far away as fast as possible."

In her haste, Stephanie had put on the skirt instead of the uniform and was now regretting it. Jack kept a hectic pace, almost a run. "Can't we slow down a little?"

"Not unless you want them to catch up with us."

Jack veered off the traveled path and headed them toward a jutting of rocks to the west. They weaved and doubled back several times, until Stephanie was sure they were lost.

By late morning, they reached the rocks and the climb was torturous. Stephanie couldn't take much more. "How far do we have to go?"

"Not much further."

Once down the opposite side, Jack stopped. "This is it!"

Stephanie looked at Jack, with confusion. "This is what?"

Jack dropped his equipment and smiled lecherously at Stephanie. "The end of the line, Stephie. It's time for us, now."

"But my father..."

"Yeah, your father. A funny thing... there were people willing to pay me more to see you never leave the jungle. So... it won't matter what shape you're in... and no one will ever know. Surprise... this is it." Jack threw up his hands.

Stephanie could hardly believe she had been so stupid. She was totally at his mercy. Her only chance, though slim, was to make a run for it.

She moved only a few feet, before Jack came crushing down on her, in a football style tackle. She put up a violent struggle, but it was pointless. He pinned her against the ground, laughing loudly and whispering obscenities in her ear. Stephanie let the fight go out of her body, hoping he would lessen his hold on her. Once her arm was free, she felt around for the hard object he had flung her hand against in the struggle. It was a heavy stone. Cautiously, she gripped the stone in her hand, gathered every once of strength and crashed the stone into his head.

The stone met his skull with a dull thud and he moaned, then lost consciousness. With some effort, Stephanie pushed his body aside. She didn't know if he was dead or only stunned. Either way, she was getting out of there fast. She didn't stop to think, just grabbed the canteen and headed back over the rocks, from where they'd come.

She wasn't at all sure she could find her way back. Michael could very well get his wish and never see her return from the jungle. Stephanie was sure he had paid Jack.

Hours passed, then Stephanie finally collapsed in tears. This was all Michael's fault. If she ever got out of this alive, she would divorce him. Stephanie fought back the tears and found her feet again. She walked in the direction she thought was right, but knew she was roaming aimlessly. She had no idea where she was or where she was going. In the day's remaining light and the beginning of the next, she traveled.

A gentle rain began to fall late that morning. Stephanie took shelter beneath the dense vines. The drops of rain fell in an almost hypnotic pattern. They patted the leaves high above her and dropped lazily to the jungle floor. They made hardly a sound when they hit the ground. The moss and rotted wood acted as a cushion, breaking each drop's fall, then soaking it up like a sponge.

Stephanie imagined herself back at home, watching the rain fall from her bedroom window. Why had she come to this country? Something had made her come here. Was it her own choosing, or had the fates planned it? Was this the way she was destined to die, lost and alone? No one to say goodbye to.

Stephanie's thinking was distorted and sluggish, from no food and no sleep. She wiped what she though was a rain drop from her cheek, when in reality, it was a tear, quickly followed by many more. The rain was brief and ended as suddenly as it began. With the end of the rain, came the end of her tears. There were none left. Stephanie had lost heart and any hope of finding her way out of the jungle. All she wanted to do was sleep. She lay her head down against the mossy ground and closed her eyes. She said a prayer, to die in her sleep... never expecting to wake.

Just as she finished her prayer, a crackling sound met her ears, causing her eyes to fly open. A man's boot appeared near her face on the ground. Stephanie jerked away, quickly, in the thought that it was Jack.

It was Amelio. He knelt near her. She was so glad to see him, she couldn't control herself. She flung her arms around him and hugged him tightly.

"It's all right... everything is all right. Tell me where Jack is."

Stephanie was giggling uncontrollably. "I... I hit him... with a stone... I might have killed him... I don't know... he didn't move."

Stephanie couldn't bring herself to let go of Amelio. He sensed her need and sat down to hold her in his arms, his face only inches from hers. The inevitable drew their lips together and unleashed a flood of passionate kisses. Stephanie had not wanted to admit her feelings for this man... but they would not be quieted now.

Amelio pulled away and back into reality. "You must be hungry. Here." Amelio gave Stephanie some bread and a piece of cheese. Stephanie accepted them eagerly.

When she was finished, Amelio stood beside her and held out his hand. "We better get back to the village. If Jack is not dead, he'll be coming after you."

Amelio held tight to Stephanie's hand along the trail. They met up with Anzo, several hours later.

"You found her... What about Jack?"

"He might be dead, but we won't take any chances. He's a pretty tough customer."

Now on the trail, they moved rapidly back to the village. When they arrived, there was much celebration at hand. The three were greeted by several of the villagers who spoke, joyously, to them in Spanish. The two men were elated by what they heard. They began to holler and jump around like small children.

Stephanie wanted to know what was going on. "What is it?"

Amelio grabbed her by the arms. "The revolution has come! We are in control of the country!"

Stephanie couldn't help but feel happy for them, but sad for herself. This meant she would be leaving.

Amelio saw the little sadness in Stephanie's eyes. He spoke to Anzo in Spanish, Anzo smiled and left them. Amelio turned to Stephanie.

"This calls for a celebration. Come. We will have some wine."

Amelio took Stephanie by the hand and led her back to the small house. He lit some candles and poured the wine. "Mrs... Stephanie, I think I can persuade them to let you go now... We will leave for the capitol tomorrow. You could be back with your family within a matter of days."

Stephanie looked down into her glass. "I won't have a family when I get back. I'm divorcing Michael, as soon as possible."

"Things may have changed..."

"No. Michael paid Jack to come back here and kill me... I could never trust him again. It is over... there's nothing left."

"What will you do?"

"Go back to the States, I guess."

Amelio walked round the table and stood behind Stephanie. "You could stay here." Amelio placed his hands on her shoulders and pulled her up from the chair. "You could stay here... with me."

The chemistry erupted volcanically. The candles flickered and danced, in the otherwise darkness, causing the lover's shadows to sway on the walls.

Anzo smiled a knowing smile at Stephanie, as they packed for the trip to the capitol. The journey was long. Over the course of their travel, they passed through many small villages, one the same as another. Poverty, sickness, and filthy conditions were prominent features. Small dirty children and animals ran the narrow streets. The children were begging for food.

The pain in her eyes at these sights was matched by Amelio's. At every village, he gave what supplies could be spared, though always sorry there was never enough.

They traveled by many different modes of transportation.

As they closed in on the capital, they secured a jeep and a military escort. Bumpy as the ride was, Stephanie was glad not to be walking. There were still isolated trouble spots and several skirmishes were fought along the way. In talking with the soldiers they met, Amelio found that Stephanie's husband had left the country during the height of the revolution, but would be returning, when things were more settled. Amelio wanted more than ever to meet this man face to face.

As the jeep crested the mountain road, the city of San Sabo lay before them. It wasn't Boston but Stephanie was very glad to see it.

General Cadeez, a stout, stern looking man, stood proudly on the steps of the presidential residence. The jeep, carrying the three, jerked to a halt at the base of the steps. Amelio led Stephanie up the steps. He embraced the general, then introduced Stephanie.

"Father..."

Stephanie was surprised to find Amelio was the son of the new President.

"... this is Stephanie Cantrel... the woman I am going to marry."

Stephanie's eyes widened with surprise, as Amelio's father's eyes narrowed, with concern. Before another word could pass between Stephanie and Amelio, the general split them up.

"I am sure the lady would like a nice hot bath, after her arduous journey."

The general called to one of the servants. "See that Mrs..." He emphasized the 'Mrs.' "Cantrel has a room, a bath and some fresh clothing. If you will excuse me, Mrs. Cantrel, I would like to speak to my son."

Stephanie sensed the general's hostility. "Of course, excuse me." Stephanie left with the maid.

152

Amelio and his father went into the library. Amelio's father closed the door. "What is the meaning of this, Amelio? Bringing the woman here!"

"But father, the revolution has come, we no longer need the money. We have control of the treasury. We are in control."

"The money is no longer an issue. We are in control, yes. And, being the new government, I am not sure the United States is going to overlook the kidnapping of one of its citizens, by the new president's son."

"I thought it was all kept quiet. No one knew who had taken her."

"That was true, until you brought her here. Now it could be made obvious that it was our doing. She'll tell the world that we were the ones that kidnapped her. It will jeopardize our relations with the U.S." The new President walked away from Amelio, then turned back to him. "It would have been better, if she had died in the jungle."

"But father, I am in love with her... and she with me. There was never any talk of killing the woman. She will not say anything."

"She will tell her husband."

"No. He sent that mercenary back to kill her..."

Amelio's father said nothing and walked away.

"It was her husband who sent him, wasn't it father? Well... wasn't it?"

"Amelio, sometimes in order to achieve a goal one must make sacrifices along the way."

"Is that what she is to you, father, a sacrifice? You are sounding like the old regime, now. What has happened to you?"

Amelio's father stood before him, and placed his hand on Amelio's shoulder. "My son, we have a cause to think of... we must not loose sight of that cause."

"It seems to me father, that you already have." Amelio jerked away from his father and stormed from the room.

Stephanie soaked her weary body in the tub of warm water. It hardly seemed possible to be in civilization again. Running water, fans, she'd never take them for granted, again. She dressed in the clothes the maid brought and lay down on the bed. A bed with a real mattress.

She fell off to sleep and was still sleeping, when Amelio entered her room, looking so different in his slacks and jacket. Softly, he sat on the bed next to her and ran his finger down her arm. It tickled and she moved a bit. He did it again and she woke. He kissed her.

"Good afternoon... or evening, as it were. It's time for dinner."

Stephanie smiled up at him. She wished she could always be wakened by his handsome, loving face.

Amelio escorted Stephanie to the table and seated her next to him. Amelio's father was polite in a strained manner. He spoke mostly to Amelio, about all the things they must now do, all the time that would be involved, all the dedication necessary and lack of time for personal interests. With every word and every glance, he made it clearer and clearer to Stephanie, that she was not welcome there... that she had no future with Amelio, nor he with her. Amelio had a duty to his country and to his people. The clincher was when he mentioned the fact that Amelio would eventually take over from him and how it would be necessary to establish a strong family alliance, with one of the respected families in Bacaba. His marriage would be a vital part of the future of their country.

Stephanie could stand no more. The message was clear. She excused herself, on the premise of being tired. As she left the room, she heard Amelio and his father begin to argue, but did not stay to listen.

Stephanie stood on the balcony, watching the stars in the clear night sky. She knew what she was imagining for Amelio and herself was but a fairy tale. Life was never so simple and direct. Where would she go from here? What direction to take? She knew she must leave.

A knock came on the door and the new president let himself in. "I am sorry to disturb you Mrs. Cantrel, but we must talk."

Stephanie put on her bravest, most serene face. "Yes, Mr. President?"

"Surely you realize that my son cannot marry you."

"Yes. You made that quite clear."

"He is a very determined young man... as long as you are within his grasp, he will not let go. You must leave."

Stephanie nodded.

"I have arranged for a car to take you to the Embassy. You're husband will be returning in a few days. Be ready first thing in the morning. Before Amelio wakes."

"I will."

"He will come to you tonight. You must not tell him of our conversation."

"I won't."

"I am glad we are in agreement on this. Good night Mrs. Cantrel."

Amelio's father left the room. About an hour later, Amelio came to her. He spoke lovingly to her and tried to smooth over his father's insistence against them. He told her he loved her, and then showed her how much.

Stephanie slipped from the bed before daybreak, dressed and was ushered into the waiting car by two uniformed guards. After several miles, it occurred to Stephanie that they were driving away from the city... away from the Embassy. Something was wrong. She eyed the two men suspiciously. Then, she felt it. They were going to kill her.

For lack of any better plan, Stephanie reached forward and grabbed the steering wheel. The car swerved as the two men tried to wrench her hands from the wheel. In the struggle, the car failed to maneuver the curve in the road and crashed over the side, downward into the ravine. The car rolled several times, before coming to rest on its top.

Dazed but conscious, Stephanie crawled out of the car, through the window, and moved clear. As she stumbled through the brush, the car exploded into flames.

Hadn't she been through enough? Here she was, in a foreign country. Her husband and the local government were both trying to kill her. There was no place to run. No refuge. She fell into the brush, as she lost consciousness.

Chapter 5

As Stephanie's eyes finally opened and tried to focus, she saw the face of a young boy, looking down at her.

"The Senora is all right?"

Stephanie raised herself up on one elbow. "Si."

"Bad accident. You much lucky lady."

Stephanie heard voices above them on the road and caught a glimpse of military uniforms. Stephanie placed her hand over the boy's mouth and pulled him down into the brush with her.

"Please, I won't hurt you. They must not find me. They will kill me. Do you understand."

The boy nodded his head and Stephanie removed her hand.

"Can you tell me what they are saying?"

"Si, Senora."

The boy listened and translated. "'... all dead... no survivors... the president will be pleased.' They are leaving, now."

Stephanie remained tense, until she heard the jeep drive away.

"Are you a bandito, Senora?"

Stephanie smiled at the boy, "No. I'm not a bandito. Just a silly woman, in love with the wrong man."

"Ah, Sedro knows all about these things." The boy pointed to himself.

"You do?"

"Si. You come with me. I will show you a place to hide."

Stephanie followed the boy through the ravine and over some hills to a small farm.

"This is where I live. My mother is working in the city, she will not be back until two days from now. You can stay here till then. Are you hungry? I could fix you something.' The boy was being an excellent host. "No, Sedro. Thank you. What about your father?"

"I cannot talk about my father, Senora. It could be dangerous for him."

"I understand. Do you know much about the city?"

"Oh, yes. I work there sometime, too. Sedro knows all places."

"You seem an enterprising young man." Stephanie reached into her pocket and pulled out her grandmother's locket.

"How would you like to have this for your mother?"

"Si, Senora. It is very beautiful. My mother would like it much. But, I must earn it honestly. My mother would insist on that."

Stephanie was impressed by the boy's loyalty to his mother's teachings. "Would you be able to take me into the city, without anyone seeing me?"

"Where in the city would you want to go?"

"The American Embassy." Stephanie, knew any chance she had left, lay within the embassy walls. Maybe she could beat Michael there and leave the country before he returned. Although, without her passport, it might be difficult.

"That is an easy job for such a beautiful necklace. I have worked, sometimes, at the embassy. Getting to the gate is not a problem. Getting you inside could be more trouble..." The boy smiled an impish smile. "but not impossible, if you were my mother. You stay here. You will be safe. I will go to the embassy and find some work for you. Sedro will handle it."

Sedro left on the run. Stephanie hoped she wasn't endangering the boy.

The little farm house was very neat though very poor. Stephanie lay on a bed near the open door and slept. Sometime after dark, Sedro returned and woke Stephanie. "Senora. It is all fixed. You must go with me to the embassy tomorrow morning."

Stephanie hugged the boy. "Thank you Sedro... here." Stephanie handed him the locket. "You take this now... just in case."

"I will take, it, but there will be no in case. Sedro will see to it. I will fix some dinner now."

The boy was most efficient, despite his small size. He prepared a simple, yet satisfying, meal. Then, he left the house to do his chores. He carried a lantern and Stephanie followed him. "I must take care of tomorrow's work, now. We will leave before daybreak."

Sedro was quite the little man. Stephanie watched him and wondered if she would ever have children. Michael thought children were a nuisance. Stephanie knew with him, she would never have a child. She didn't feel she would even want his child. But Amelio... she could have Amelio's child. She almost hoped their night of passion had planted a seed of love to grow within her. If she couldn't have the man... maybe she could have his child.

Sedro directed Stephanie to take the bed in the back room, just to be safe. The back room was really only the back of the house, where some blankets had been draped from a rope. "This is my mother's bed. She would not mind, if you used it. She would like you. You sleep now. We must leave early."

Stephanie lay awake in the small bed, dreaming of Amelio and wishing to be with him.

Next morning, Sedro entered her room, with the lantern. "Time to wake up, Senora."

He set about picking some clothes from his mothers sparse wardrobe. "Here is a shawl, you must wear it over your head and put this apron over your skirt."

Stephanie followed the small boy with the lantern, out into the predawn.

"If we meet anyone on the way, keep your head down and do not look up. I will do all the talking. See?"

Stephanie nodded. Sedro's pace was quick and his footing sure on the darkened road. Surprisingly, there were many others on the road. All on their way to the city to work. They traveled down many back streets, once in the city proper. The sun was lifting over the horizon and everything was bathed in early morning glow. A military truck turned down the street they were on. Sedro pushed Stephanie into a dark doorway, till they were past. Sedro had learned even at his tender age, to survive in this country torn by unrest.

They reached the gates of the embassy, without incident. Sedro spoke to the guard and they were allowed inside the compound. Sedro opened the door to the embassy and approached the man at the front desk. "Senior Rigby."

"Sedro. Hello. You're a bit early, but you and your mother go ahead to the kitchen."

"No Senior. The lady is not my mother. She is a surprise for you."

Rigby rose quickly to his feet. "What the..."

Stephanie lowered the shawl, removed it, and wrapped it and the apron together. She handed them to Sedro. "Thank you so much, Sedro. You are a brave little man." She kissed him on the cheek. He seemed embarrassed, said goodbye, and left the embassy.

The man behind the desk was still in shock, at the boy having penetrated the embassy with an impostor. "Well... Who are you and what business have you here?"

"I am Stephanie Cantrel... I believe you were expecting me some weeks ago."

"Mrs. Cantrel..." The man seemed to be looking at a ghost. "... We received word just last evening that... that you were dead."

"As someone once said 'the rumors of my death are greatly exaggerated'. Is my husband here?"

"No... He is enroute. We've already notified him of your... death. He will be quite shocked."

"I bet he will. My clothes were sent on ahead, before I was... detained. Are they here somewhere?"

"Uh... Yes ma'am. Here. I'll show you."

The man showed her to a room on the second floor, overlooking the garden.

Stephanie washed and changed her clothes, then went back to Rigby's desk.

Stephanie had decided to confront Michael. "Rigby, isn't it?"

"Yes ma'am."

"Please don't say anything to my husband, when he arrives. I would rather surprise him."

"I would dare say he will be surprised."

"I'll wait in his office, if I may?"

"Right through those doors, ma'am."

Rigby pointed her in the right direction. She entered and closed the doors. Deliberately, she positioned herself in the big chair in front of the desk, so Michael would not see her as he entered. After about a half hour, Rigby brought her a cup of coffee and the news that her husband's plane had landed. He would be there within the hour. Stephanie used the time to go over in her mind all the things she would say to him.

Voices floated in from the outer hall. She heard Rigby telling Michael he had a visitor in his office. Stephanie flinched slightly, as the door opened and she heard his footsteps cross the room to the desk. He placed his brief case on the desk, then looked across to the visitor. Shock and horror filled his face., He went white pale. "Stephanie..." He swallowed hard. "... is it really you?"

"Yes, Michael. It's really me. Surprised? If you paid any money before he completed the job, you were cheated."

"What are you talking about?"

"Come on, Michael. You wouldn't pay the ransom... They were going to kill me, if Daddy hadn't agreed to pay it. But then you decided you didn't want me to come back and paid him to make sure of it." Stephanie's eyes were cold and filled with contempt.

"Stephanie, I'm very confused. I paid the ransom. The State Department helped me get it. Then I didn't hear anymore, till the new government informed me that you'd been killed in an accident, on being returned to the capitol. The new regime rescued you, but were fired upon, as they entered the city. The car went off the road and exploded... No one survived the crash." Michael fell into his chair, looking a bit ill. "But here you are alive. You say they got money from your father, too? He didn't say anything to me about it."

Michael's expression changed as the last thing Stephanie said hit home in his mind. "You think I paid someone to kill you? Is that what you said?"

Stephanie made no response, but sat watching Michael's expressions. "How could you believe such a thing, Stephanie? You are my wife." Michael got up and walked around the room, then turned and stood beside Stephanie. "Are you all right? Did they... harm you in any way? Do you know who they were? The names on the passenger list were fake and no one could give a good description."

Stephanie continued to sit in silence, confused. Maybe she'd been wrong? Michael placed his hand on her shoulder. "I'm glad you're all right." He leaned over and kissed her on the cheek.

"Come. We'll have breakfast in the garden." Michael offered his arm to Stephanie and escorted her to the garden.

The table had already been set. When the food arrived, Stephanie marveled at the fact that it was more food than she'd seen in weeks. She was decidedly hungry. "So, Stephanie. Tell me everything. They really parachuted you from the plane into the jungle?"

"Yes. It was frightening. But I must admit, a little exciting. I'd never want to relive it though."

Michael leaned toward her. "What happened down in the jungle? Did they... molest you?" Michael's tone was almost voyeuristic. His eyes showed a strange excitement at anticipation of her answer.

Stephanie looked down into her plate. "I'd rather not discuss that right now."

Michael leaned back in his chair, changing back to the ever so proper gentleman he always presented. "Later then. Would you be able to recognize any of them? Would there be any chance of our apprehending them?"

Stephanie felt something strange in these questions and the questions from the office. It was, as if he were simply asking the appropriate questions and not necessarily expecting answers. There were already several questions asked that she hadn't even acknowledged. Yet he didn't seem concerned at not having an answer.

"No, I doubt that I could recognize them." Stephanie lied, because to identify Jack was to identify Amelio... and she could never do that.

Michael reached over and touched her hand. His hand was cold. "Darling, you finish your breakfast. I have some work I must attend to. Oh, I'll cable your father you are all right. And I'll call the doctor. Have him check you over."

"Doctor? I don't think..."

"You really should have him take a look at you. You could have contracted some contagious disease or something out there."

Stephanie detected that his concern was more for himself than for her. "All right."

Stephanie remained confused. Had Michael really paid the ransom or was this all an act? His tone with her was just as condescending and artificial as it had always been. But maybe he wasn't totally heartless. Maybe he didn't wish her dead. Stephanie rested most of the afternoon after the doctor left, declaring her weak, but otherwise healthy. She dressed for dinner and Michael appeared at the door to escort her down. Appearances were important to Michael. Everything always had to look "right", no matter what.

Dinner was quiet, just the embassy staff. That was more than enough for Stephanie, as they were loaded with questions about her ordeal. They all left the table, however, with longing looks in their eyes. All hungry for more details than Stephanie would divulge.

Stephanie changed for bed. It felt good to wear her own clothes, sleep in a bed she could call her own, and rest with some feeling of safety. She climbed into bed with a book to read. A soft knock came at the door. "Yes?"

"May I come in?"

"Yes, Michael."

Michael came to the bed and sat near Stephanie. "Now is the time, Stephanie, for you to tell me what they did to you." Michael stroked her arm as he spoke. "I won't be able to... understand... when there is a... problem, if you don't confide in me. You must tell me."

Michael's eyes had that same strange look from breakfast. Stephanie wondered why he was so sure something had happened. What did he know, that he wasn't telling her? She swallowed hard. She must tell him something... or he would not be satisfied. She was too well aware of his persistent doggedness, when he wanted something. Stephanie placed the book on the table, folded her hands on her lap and looked down at them.

"Well, Michael. One of them was not very nice to me... he tried to rape me and he was... going to kill me." Stephanie looked up at Michael, for some response.

"Is that the one you thought I sent to... to kill you?"

"Yes... I may have killed him. I hit him... with a rock and he didn't get up after that. He may be dead."

Another funny look that Stephanie couldn't identify crossed Michael's face. He put his arm around her. "If he is dead... he deserves to be dead. I am sorry you were put though all this. Luckily, he didn't accomplish what he had planned. You are safe now. What about the others? The report said there were three of them."

"They didn't hurt me. One was even nice to me." Stephanie would never tell Michael just how nice Amelio had been.

"It's all over now." Michael kissed her cheek, then her neck. Stephanie sensed he was going to make love to her. Michael seemed excited by what had happened to her. She didn't want Michael. She wanted Amelio... but she was married to Michael. Michael turned off the light.

Chapter 6

Michael left the embassy late the next afternoon. He indicated to Stephanie that he would not be back until very late. The meeting might even last till morning. Stephanie made no inquiry as to whom he was going to see. If she had, she would have found that his meeting was with the new president and his cabinet.

Just before dinner, Stephanie took a walk around the compound. She stood at the big iron gates, watching the people going by in the street. After a moment, she noticed a man leaning against the wall in an alleyway across the street, a little east of the gate. As her eyes found him, he removed his hat and smoothed back his blonde hair. It was Jack! He wasn't dead! The sight of him uncapped a well of terror. Stephanie stumbled back inside the embassy.

"Mrs. Cantrel." Ribgy rose from his seat. "Are you all right? Should I call for the doctor?"

"No... no. I'll be all right." Stephanie spent the rest of the day in her room, too afraid to venture out.

Michael's meeting broke for dinner at the president's house. The president gave Michael a seat of honor near him and introduced Michael to his son, Amelio. The president put on his most sympathetic expression. "Mr. Ambassador, I am sorry we did not get a chance to speak before the meeting. And I am most distressed at your recent loss. I am sure your wife was most precious to you. You do appear to be handling it very well."

"Strange thing about that, Mr. President. It seems there was some sort of mix up. My wife is fine. When I arrived, she was waiting for me at the embassy."

Amelio choked on his wine. His previously morose expression was replaced by surprise, then anger.

"I apologize for the confusion, Ambassador. There was much confusion during the first few days of our takeover. I can only attribute the inaccurate report to that confusion. Has your wife been able to shed any light on the identity of her captors?"

The president looked expectant.

"No. I'm afraid not. She said she could not recognize them. I suspect she has some kind of subconscious block against remembering. She told me that one of them treated her badly. They told her I never paid the ransom which is utterly ridiculous, as I know very well I did. Her mind is muddled. She seems to think I paid one of them to kill her. I've already consulted a local psychiatrist on her behalf. She will need therapy for a time, but I will see that she gets the best of care. After all... she is my wife."

The words Michael spoke did not match his expression. The words were caring, but the expression was remote and uninvolved. Amelio watched Michael intently and was very aware of the contradiction.

Amelio met with his father after dinner, before the meeting resumed. He was outraged. "You... *you* ordered her killed, didn't you? Twice! First Jack and then the soldiers. I saw your face when he said she was still alive. She has out maneuvered you father! I told you she would not betray me. She loves me."

"Amelio. Don't talk nonsense. I'm glad she is all right. But she has obviously made her choice. She is with her husband, as it should be. You heard him. He is going to see

166

that she gets the best of care. Leave it alone and get on with your life."

"He does not care for her. I could see it in his eyes."

"She knows her place, Amelio, and it is not with you." Amelio's father marched from the room.

Michael returned to the embassy shortly after 2:00 am, to find Stephanie sitting in her room in the dark. "Stephanie are you all right? Mary says you did not come down to dinner."

"Michael... I want to go back to the States."

"Nonsense. Your place is here with me."

"Michael, please."

"Stephanie... What is wrong?"

"I'm afraid to be here."

"That's only natural, after all you've been through. You're perfectly safe here at the embassy. No one can harm you here."

"I want a divorce, Michael."

"For what reason? On what grounds?" Michael was calm.

"You don't love me Michael. You never have."

"You knew that in the beginning. You do not love me... I accept that."

"But, Michael..."

Michael pulled Stephanie up from the chair, resting his hands solidly on both her shoulders. "Listen to me carefully, Stephanie. I will only tell you this once and we will not discuss it again. I will not let you leave and I will never... allow you to divorce me. Now, you are my wife, you will remain my wife, and you will conduct yourself in a manner befitting my wife. That is the end of it."

Stephanie started to protest, but realized the futility of it. She had a better understanding now of why Michael had been so insistent about her coming here with him. She was his prisoner. She could not escape him here. She had no passport and only Michael could get her another. There was no one to turn to for help. He could control her here. Looking into his cold blue eyes told her just how serious he was about never letting her go. He hadn't spoken it, but she felt him think it. He'd see her dead first.

Next morning, Michael was gone early. There was a note folded on Stephanie's breakfast plate. Stephanie opened it and her heart iced, as she read the words. "If you venture outside the embassy, I will be waiting. I am watching you. Our time together is still to come."

Jack... it was Jack. He was not going to leave her alone. How did he get inside the embassy? How could he get so close to her, without anyone knowing? Who could she turn to? Who could she tell? If she told Michael, she might put Amelio in jeopardy. Amelio was the only bastion of hope she had in this country. If she could just speak to him, maybe he would know what to do. She could not send him a note through the embassy staff; Michael would find out. The embassy calls were monitored. She couldn't venture outside... Jack could be waiting for her. Stephanie's current dilemma seemed hopeless. So much so, she tried to forget it by busying her mind with reading and puzzles and card games. They were only mildly effective.

Stephanie found she could not stomach dinner. She went to her room, took a bath, and soaked a long time. She stepped out of the bath and put on her robe. Still deeply worried, she sat at her vanity, combing her hair. There in the mirror was his face... Jack... clear and vivid.

Petrified, she sat motionless for what seemed an eternity. Finally, she turned to face him, but he was gone. She ran out into the hall. No one was there. She ran to the stairs. There was no one at the entrance except Rigby sitting at his desk busy with paperwork.

"Rigby?" Stephanie called to him loudly. "Did you see anyone come down the stairs?"

"No, Mrs. Cantrel."

"Is there anyone but embassy personnel on the grounds?"

"No ma'am... is something wrong?"

"Uh... no... no. I must have fallen asleep and had a dream. I'm sorry to have bothered you." Stephanie tried to brush the whole thing off.

"That's OK, Mrs. Cantrel. I would imagine it would be hard to forget all you've been through. Nightmares are probably normal."

"Yes, well... is Mr. Cantrel back yet?"

"No, ma'am. He said it could be quite late."

"Well, thank you. Goodnight."

"Goodnight, Mrs. Cantrel."

Rigby watched as she returned to her room, then went back to his work.

Stephanie thought, pensively. Could she have imagined it? Was she so paranoid, now, about Jack that she would see him around every corner, in every mirror, in her dreams? Would he haunt her forever? But it had been so real. How could she have imagined it?

Stephanie lay in bed, unable to sleep. The door knob turned slowly as Stephanie lay fearful of who might be on the other side. The door opened.

"Stephanie, are you asleep?" Michael spoke in a low voice.

Stephanie sighed in relief. "No, I'm not asleep."

Michael stood by the bed, holding a cup in his hand. "How are you feeling?"

"Fine... Just fine."

"Now, if you were fine, you would be asleep. Here. I had Mary make you an herbal tea. It will help you relax."

Stephanie took the cup and sipped the bitter sweet liquid.

"Drink it down. It may not taste the greatest, but a good night's sleep will make it worth while. Goodnight... darling." Michael kissed her on the forehead and left the room.

"Darling?" Stephanie said it to herself. Why had he suddenly begun to call her "darling"? He never called her that before. He'd been using the term toward her, ever since he arrived. Darling? Stephanie found the term annoying, because it was such an outrageous lie.

The effects of the tea moved easily over Stephanie, like a soft summer breeze. Her body yielded to its comfort and warmth. Her eyes closed and she slept. Some sound or movement caused her to force open her eyes. It was difficult, for her lids felt laden with some heavy weight.

The room moved and waved, as if under water, and the moon lit the room with an eerie light. Near the bed stood a large dark figure. The figure moved nearer.

Panic and terror caused a scream to rise to Stephanie's lips, as the figure's face came clearer. Jack!

He spoke to her. "It's our time."

She screamed again, but still could not hear her scream. He reached for her. This time she heard her scream and sat up. In an effort to block out the vision, she placed her hands over her face. She heard running footsteps and someone touched her. She was afraid to look.

"Stephanie... Stephanie, what is it?"

Slowly, she moved her hands from her eyes. "Michael... he was here!"

"Who was here, Stephanie? Who?"

"The man that tried to kill me... Jack." She had not meant to speak his name.

"There is no one here, Stephanie."

"But, he was here."

"No, Stephanie. You dreamt it."

Several of the staff were standing in the doorway. Michael spoke to them. "Rigby, call Dr. Cordova. The rest of you go back to bed. Just lie down Stephanie and try to relax."

"But I'm sure."

"It was just a bad dream."

The doctor sedated Stephanie. Michael took the doctor into his office and closed the door.

"Dr. Cordova, I am worried about my wife. I think she is very near a nervous collapse. She is overreacting, jumpy and sometimes makes no sense at all. I think they may have done something... unspeakable to her and she feels too guilty and ashamed to speak of it. She seems most depressed and I'm afraid... she might try to... kill herself."

The doctor was mildly surprised. "I had no idea she was so upset. Mr. Cantrel, your wife has been through a terrible ordeal. There are bound to be some residual effects. It is important to reassure her, and make her feel safe here. I will prescribe some tranquilizers and sleeping pills. It is all going to take some time. But, if things are as bad with her as you say, I think you should consult a psychiatrist."

Michael was all too pleased with the doctor's recommendation, as if it were something he'd been working toward. "Thank you, Dr. Cordova. I will do that."

Stephanie remained on medication and was placed under the care of a psychiatrist, but stayed at the embassy. After several weeks of intensive counseling, Stephanie was convinced that her visions of the man called Jack were all in her subconscious. Despite the fact that Stephanie had not confided everything to the counselor, she had begun to feel better... less frightened.

It was Friday when the psychiatrist made his last visit. He met with Michael after speaking briefly with Stephanie.

"Mr. Cantrel, I think it would be a good idea to take your wife on an outing... maybe shopping. She needs to get out and be around other people, in order to help her regain her confidence. She feels very vulnerable and she is still apprehensive. Don't make it a long outing... maybe a few hours. Convince her that she is safe with you and with others. Unless any further problems develop, I won't see Stephanie, again here at the embassy. If she wants to see me, she'll come to my office."

"What if there is a relapse?"

"Then I think we may need to hospitalize her. But, if you take it slow and don't push her, I don't think that will be necessary."

"Thank you, doctor. I'll arrange a shopping trip for tomorrow."

After the doctor was shown from the embassy, Michael went to Stephanie, in her room. He knocked, then entered.

"Stephanie, the doctor says you are ready for the outside world. I have arranged for you to do some shopping in the morning. You know how you like to shop. Then we could have lunch out somewhere. All right?"

Stephanie managed a meager smile and agreed. She had been thinking alot about Amelio lately. Michael was an intrusion on those thoughts. Amelio must know, by now, that Stephanie was at the embassy. Why hadn't he made any attempt to reach her? Had he rethought his feelings? She still loved him... she felt she always would, even if they could never be together. Maybe it was her fate to be tied to Michael. He really never treated her badly. He saw to all her needs... in his own way. Maybe she should try harder to be what he wanted her to be. Maybe then she could live her life instead of always fighting it. But, the thought of submission was repugnant to Stephanie. Michael was her jailer and she his prisoner. If nothing else, she had realized that in her counseling. Michael represented an obstacle to her own fulfillment. But that obstacle was unmoving and unyielding as a block of granite.

Stephanie was nervous about leaving the compound. Yet with each passing moment, her confidence grew and her fear diminished. As they shopped the many stalls and booths in the Plaza, Stephanie found herself looking over her shoulder and into dark corners in anticipation of the "Jack-in-the-box".

By lunch, she hardly thought about Jack at all. They finished lunch and left the restaurant for the waiting car. Michael searched his pockets for something. "Oh, dear."

"What is it, Michael?"

"I left my wallet on the table. Wait here, I'll be right back."

"But..."

Michael walked away, quickly, leaving Stephanie feeling naked on the sidewalk, with people walking all around her. She tried desperately to hold onto her composure, not to panic. However, the panic began to well up from the dark recesses where she'd plunged it only hours before. When the hand touched her arm, she felt faint. She didn't want to see, but she forced herself to look. Tears of relief and joy flooded her face, as the boy, Sedro, stood at her elbow.

"Senora... How are you? You look sick... Are you sick, Senora?"

Stephanie placed her hand to his cheek. "No, Sedro, I'm not sick. I'm just fine. What have you been doing?"

"Looking for work, Senora, as always."

Stephanie mopped the tears from her face with a hanky and Michael, again stood beside her. "What's the matter with you?'"

Stephanie smiled. "Oh, nothing. I'd like you to meet someone. This is Sedro. He's the young man who helped me find my way to the embassy. He's looking for some work. Don't you think we could find some work for him at the embassy, Michael?" Stephanie's look was pleading.

Michael looked down disdainfully at the grubby boy. Stephanie urged him. "Please Michael. I owe him my life."

Michael looked away in a disinterest manner. "I guess we can find something. I'll speak to Rigby."

Michael looked down at the boy again and spoke in a curt manner. "Report to the embassy Monday morning, boy."

"Thank you, senior and thank you, senora."

The boy ran off down the street, kicking up his heals and laughing. Stephanie touched Michael's arm. "Thank you, Michael." Michael's eyes were void of emotion. They climbed into the car and drove back to the embassy.

Stephanie changed, put away her new found treasures and met Michael in the garden for an early dinner.

"Stephanie, now that I've done you a favor, I would like you to do one for me."

"What is it?"

"There is a dinner party at the president's home tomorrow evening. I would like you to accompany me."

"But, Michael... I'm not sure I could handle it."

"You'll handle it, Stephanie. It is important to me."

Stephanie hesitated, yet agreed.

Chapter 7

Stephanie was more apprehensive about her reaction to seeing Amelio than she was about being among all those strangers. In frustration, she changed her clothes at least 5 times, before settling on an elaborately detailed, beaded, blue gown. She looked at herself a long time in the full length mirror. It had been months since she had attended an official function. She was pleased at how nice she looked. Amelio... He had never seen her like this. What would his reaction be? Did he still care about her, or had that been the passion of the moment? Stephanie held herself in her arms and fantasized about dancing with Amelio... having him hold her in his strong arms... escaping to him.

She looked up at herself in the mirror, startled. The realization that once she and Amelio touched, she would not be able to control her feelings for him and keep herself in check, struck her like a freight train, devastating her. She would not be able to be near him, let alone dance with him. She must avoid him at all cost, lest she betray her feelings... and him.

Michael walked into the room, without knocking. Stephanie turned, quickly in surprise. "I'm sorry. I didn't mean to frighten you. My, my! You look... elegant. I'm proud of the way you've risen to this occasion. We have our differences, and I realize this is not the life you want. But, I appreciate the fact that you do think of my side of things... Sometimes I wish things could be different between us. In time, here, with no outside influences, maybe it can be."

Michael's sincerity was questionable in Stephanie's mind. His words did however, reinforce her understanding that she was his prisoner, in this country, and she had no real choices.

"Now come. I've had my car brought round. It will be just the two of us."

They were not the first nor the last to arrive. They were fashionably... in the middle. They were announced at the door and greeted by their host, the president. His eyes lay heavily upon Stephanie. She felt their weight crushing her.

"Ambassador Cantrel. How good of you to come. And, this must be your lovely wife."

The president took her hand and kissed it. Stephanie tried to hide her revulsion. "She is most beautiful. I would keep a close eye on her this evening, lest someone steal her away."

Michael smiled, pleased by the president's appreciation of his possession. Stephanie knew that was all she'd ever been and all she ever would be to Michael... a possession, something he could show off. Something to make him feel important. Something to use to his advantage.

"Thank you Mr. President. I will."

Stephanie eyed the crowd in the large hall. She did not see Amelio. They mingled and mixed with the rest of the guests. Michael paraded his "trophy" around the room just the way he'd always done. But this time, Stephanie could barely tolerate it. She was a non-person to Michael... without feelings to be considered. All Michael's conversations were exclusive of her save for the initial introduction.

Stephanie was relieved when the call to dinner was made and the guests were herded into the dining hall. The tables were elaborately set with much silver and crystal. Stephanie couldn't help but see the contrast between this type of dining and the meager fare that most of the country was forced to accept.

Amelio had told her of all the changes the revolution was going to bring about. Stephanie wondered how long, if ever, before those changes began.

Michael's and Stephanie's place cards were at the president's table. As the guests took their seats, the president made a toast and the dinner was begun. There was an empty chair beside the president and, beside that, a chair occupied by a lovely, young woman of that country. Stephanie decided the empty chair belonged to Amelio. The young woman she wondered about. Could she be Amelio's new love?

She hadn't long to wonder, as Amelio approached the table, in a bit of a rush. "I am sorry I am late. I had some state matters to attend to."

Stephanie's heart pounded at the sound of his voice. As her eyes met his, it was all she could do to stay in her chair... all she could do not to speak his name. The president began to introduce Amelio around the table. There were several other couples at the table and they were addressed first. Then Michael was introduced again.

"Ambassador Cantrel, I believe you have already met my son. And Mrs. Cantrel, this is my son, Amelio."

Stephanie nodded, not allowing her eyes to meet his again. Amelio sat.

"I would like, also, to take this opportunity to introduce Elaina Dernova, of the much celebrated Dernova family."

Stephanie waited for the rest of it, but there was nothing more said. All through the meal, she prayed that Amelio would not speak directly to her. At the end of the meal she was relieved he had not.

The president invited all his guests to join him in the ballroom. Michael had never been much of a dancer. He spun Stephanie around the floor one time, spotted a group of men at the far side of the room, and excused himself.

"Michael... Don't leave me alone... please."

"Nonsense, Stephanie. I must have a few words with the Minister of Defense. I won't be long." Stephanie knew all too well, that he would be gone for hours. He would always leave her to fend for herself, expecting her to make blithe conversation with the wives of the "who's who" at these affairs. In the past she had managed, though just barely at times, to do this. But, things were different now. Stephanie felt self-conscious, as if everyone were looking at her. She found her way into the garden. Her heart wanted Amelio to come to her, to carry her away, back to the jungle, anywhere away from here. Her head told her heart not to invite trouble.

The young woman that sat next to Amelio at dinner, joined Stephanie in the garden. "Mrs. Cantrel?"

"Yes."

"We were somewhat introduced. If you do not remember, my name is Elaina Dernova."

"Yes. I remember." Stephanie felt awkward.

The young woman moved closer to Stephanie. "Mrs. Cantrel... may I speak plainly?"

Stephanie was surprised, but assured the woman that she might speak. "Yes, please do."

"You are the one Amelio is in love with, are you not?"

The question, though insightful, came as a complete shock to Stephanie. She hardly knew how to respond. "I... I'm sorry."

"Amelio... You are the woman he is in love with."

Stephanie walked away. "I don't know what you are talking about. I hardly know the president's son."

Elaina, again, approached Stephanie. "It is all right. I really don't need an answer. I could see it, in the way he looked at you during dinner... and when we were dancing. Amelio's father wishes Amelio to marry me. If he were to ask me, I would marry him. Not because I love him, but because it would be my duty to my family. They wish it. I do not love Amelio. And, it is not my wish to marry him."

Stephanie could barely keep her tears in check.

"I love someone else, also. It would be very unhappy for me to be married to Amelio and be in love with someone else. In seeing you with your husband, I suspect you are finding it very unhappy, yourself. You must, of course, make your own decisions. Amelio's father is a most formidable man. He does not give up easily. It would be dangerous for you to keep loving Amelio... very dangerous."

The woman stood close behind Stephanie, now. She placed her hand on Stephanie's shoulder and spoke to her in a whisper. "As for me, I could never stop loving Salazar... no matter what the cost. I am confident in the fact, that Amelio will never ask me to marry him. He is too much in love with you. He is not happy without you. He thinks about you often. I can see it. I see his eyes look at me but they are seeing you. I thought you had a right to know how things are. I saw the hurt in your eyes, the yearning for him. I could not stand by and say nothing. If I have upset you, I am very sorry. I must go."

The woman kissed Stephanie on the cheek, then returned to the ballroom. Elaina's words echoed and reechoed in Stephanie's mind. She knew there was no hope for Amelio and herself. She couldn't even think about it.

Stephanie composed herself and returned to the ballroom, hoping to find Michael done with his conversation. He was not. The small group of men were thoroughly engrossed in their conversation. Michael didn't even notice she was standing near him. Impatiently, she tugged at his sleeve. "Michael... Michael."

"Not now, Stephanie, please. This is important. Go find someone to dance with."

Anger rose in Stephanie's cheeks. How dare he brush her off that way, after all she'd been through. She hadn't wanted to come to this party. She did it for him. He was still as selfish as ever when it came to his career. She wanted to leave. She would leave... with or without him.

Stephanie edged her way through the crowd toward the entry hall. She passed the library on her way out. A man's voice called to her and she stopped.

"Mrs. Cantrel, leaving so soon?"

The president stood in the doorway to the library. He stepped toward her and took her arm. "Join me in a drink, Mrs. Cantrel."

"No, I don't think so."

"But, I insist."

"Let go of me or I will scream."

"No. I don't think you will scream. It would embarrass your husband."

"I don't care."

"Ah, but then you would have to explain. Am I to conclude that you no longer care about Amelio?"

Stephanie didn't answer.

"Come." The president looked to see that no one was watching, pushed Stephanie into the library, and closed the door, locking it behind them. He smiled. "Just so we won't be disturbed."

The president poured two drinks and stood before Stephanie, one in each hand. "My dear. You were either born under a lucky star or you are part cat, with nine lives. You have managed to survive, when you should not have."

"I would expect you are disappointed I didn't die in the crash, or by being shot by your guards. Oh, excuse me. That would have been 'shot by factions of the old regime' wouldn't it?"

The president offered the drink to Stephanie and she refused. He downed one drink, placing the empty glass back on the tray. "Why would I want to see harm come to you?"

"Let's drop the game shall we? Tell me what you want."

"What makes you think I want anything?"

Stephanie crossed her arms. "I don't like this game."

"Ah, but games can be fun. All right, have it your way. I want your promise that you will not encourage Amelio."

"I have done nothing to encourage him. I haven't even spoken to him."

"Not yet. But can I trust you not to do so, in the future?"

Stephanie remained silent.

"No. I do not think I can trust you. I could have your husband sent out of the country and then you would be gone also."

"You would ruin his career!"

"His career is of little importance to me. My son is what is important to me... my son and his sons."

"Creating a little dynasty are we Mr. President? I thought the revolution wanted to do away with inherited right of rule. I thought they wanted free elections."

"There will be free elections... in time. You are an intelligent woman Mrs. Cantrel, maybe too intelligent for your own good. I could have you killed at any time."

Stephanie smiled at his half threat. "Yes. But Amelio would know and he would never forgive you."

"Then what am I to do with you, Mrs. Cantrel?"

"You are going to unlock the door and let me leave. I have no interest in bringing harm to your son. I am leaving this place. I want to go back to the embassy. That is what you want isn't it? For me to be out of his sight."

The president, again, lay his eyes heavy on her. "I hope we will not require another conversation, Mrs. Cantrel."

"I can't think of anything more revolting than the prospect of another conversation with you." Stephanie threw her head back in a defiant manner. She could hear the man grinding his teeth as he unlocked the door. He first checked the hallway, then allowed Stephanie to leave.

Amelio watched from an upstairs window as Stephanie slid behind the wheel of the car and passed through the gates. Cautiously, Stephanie drove down the winding mountain road. Some miles down the mountain, the car began to sputter, then the engine died. She made several fruitless attempts to restart it, then checked the gas gauge and found the tank empty. It was hard to believe Michael would be so careless. Her choice was an uphill climb back to the president's home or a downhill walk to the city. There were too many reasons not to go back to the house. She opted for the easier walk, downward. High heels proved not to be amenable to walking over this uneven road.

As she turned a curve in the road and her car was blocked from view, she heard another car winding down the road. The car's headlights glared from behind her. Fear of the unknown driver behind the wheel tugged at her heart, as she moved to the side of the road. Fearfully, she watched, as the car drew nearer. It slowed, then stopped a few feet ahead of her. The passenger's door opened and Stephanie walked toward the car. The driver was only a silhouette in the starlight. She reached the door and looked inside. "Amelio..."

Amelio smiled broadly. "Get in."

Stephanie hesitated.

"I'm not going to bite you. Get in."

Stephanie got in the car, staying close to her door, as she closed it.

"Stephanie. I wanted to speak with you so much, all evening." Amelio slid across the seat, gathered Stephanie into his arms, and kissed her passionately. She had no will to resist him. Amelio sighed. "It's so good to touch you, to taste you." Amelio kissed her again, then slid back under the wheel and threw the car into gear. "We have a lot to talk about."

"Where are we going?'"

"A place I know. It will be all right.."

"What about your father and Michael... and my car?"

"No one will know. Anzo is bringing your car down. He'll leave it for you where no one will see it."

"Anzo? You drained the gas from the car?"

"It was a risk. We had an elaborate plan to get your husband out of the way... but we didn't need it!"

"Amelio. We really shouldn't be doing this..." Stephanie smiled. "... but I can't help myself." Stephanie felt like a small child at Christmas, full of anticipation.

Amelio stopped the car at the end of a long winding dirt road, in front of a small thatched roofed house. Amelio stepped round the car, opened the door, and pulled Stephanie up into his arms. The electricity between them had not faded. If anything, it was more intense. He kissed her over and over, under a night sky full of bright stars.

He guided her inside the small house. The house was dark. Amelio left her near the door and lit some candles. It reminded Stephanie of that first night in the little hut, in Valdez. Amelio too, experienced the remembrance. The candle light flickered in Stephanie's eyes. Amelio stepped toward her. "It's almost like the first time, isn't it Stephanie?"

Like the "knight in shining armor" of her romantic fantasies, he stood before her. He cupped her face in his hands. "I love you very much, Stephanie. Nothing and no one can change that fact." His hands moved gently down her neck to her shoulders. They continued over her shoulders and down her arms, taking with them the straps of her gown. His soft kisses traveled from her brow to her waiting lips. Stephanie's body trembled with excitement and anticipation, as the beaded blue gown slipped to the floor. Amelio's body pressed gently against her's and his lips touched her shoulder. He pulled down her hair and whispered in her ear. "I love you." Their lips exploded with passionate kisses.

Amelio carried her to the small bed near the back of the house. Stephanie became drunk on the passion and never once thought of the consequences they might both have to pay for this fiery moment.

Their bodies glistened with the heat of their passion, as she lay in his arms, accepting his tender after kisses.

"Oh, Stephanie. I never want to let you go."

"And I never want to go. But we both know we can't have what we want."

"Are you still going to divorce Michael?"

"He has made that impossible. I can't even leave the country. I have no passport and he will not get me another. He has made it very clear, that he will never allow me to divorce him."

"You know my father wants me to marry Elaina. She is a nice girl, but I do not love her and she does not love me. It is not what either of us want. It is what my father expects."

Amelio stroked Stephanie's face. "I am sorry for placing you in such peril, Stephanie. But I simply cannot live without loving you. I regret taking you from the plane, for the hardship it caused you. But... I am glad, for the fact that I might otherwise never have known you. I believe in fate and our fates are mated. It will be dangerous for both of us. We must be very careful, but we can see each other.

Anzo will help. It will only be temporary. We will find a way to be together always. Even if I have to leave my country to be with you... I would do it willingly."

"Amelio... I love you."

There were so many things to say, so many thing to talk about, but there wasn't enough time. "We must go now. I'll take you to your car."

They dressed and Amelio drove Stephanie to her car. Parting was difficult, neither of them able to let go of the other. "I really must get back to the embassy, Amelio."

"I know ."

They indulged in one last lingering kiss, then Stephanie drove back to the embassy and Amelio back to his home.

Amelio's father was waiting for him. "Amelio!" His voice was angry. "Where have you been?"

"Out for a drive. I could not take any more of your party."

"It was offensive to leave Elaina here, alone."

"Father, I told Elaina I was going. She understood."

Amelio turned to go to his room, but his father caught him by the arm. "I do not understand, Amelio. Make me understand."

"You are my father. But something has happened to you. You are not the man I looked up to, as a great leader, a man of the people, a man who would reform this country's inequities. I no longer know you. You are a stranger to me. You have no reverence for life, for people. You think only of your power."

"You were with her! How dare you disobey me!"

"You have no power over me any longer. You are not my president, you are not my general, and you are no longer my father. You betrayed my trust in you... our people's trust in you. I have no respect for you."

"She has turned you against me. I'll..."

"You'll do nothing to harm her. Nothing!" Amelio left his father standing in the hall.

Though the scene between Amelio and his father was unpleasant, the scene about to erupt at the embassy would far surpass it.

Stephanie entered the embassy and rushed straight to her room. She flipped on the light and found Michael sitting in the chair near her bed. "Where have you been?"

Stephanie closed the door. "Driving."

"You embarrassed me by behaving that way."

"I told you I wanted to leave... I had to leave... You wouldn't." Stephanie started to undress. She avoided looking at Michael.

"You are having an affair aren't you?"

"Michael, how could I possibly be having an affair? This is only the second time I've left the embassy. Both times I went with you... and at your request."

"It's from before, when you were supposedly kidnapped." Michael grabbed her arm and yanked her around to face him. "What were you planning to do... fake your kidnapping, get me to pay the money and then run off with him? I'm glad I never paid the ransom." Michael hadn't meant to let that slip.

"So, it's true. You were going to let them kill me. But when my father said he'd pay... you had to stop me being turned loose. You knew all along about Jack didn't you? And you paid him... to kill me."

A look of realization spread over Stephanie's face. "Jack was here. You let him in."

Stephanie tried to think why. "You were trying to drive me crazy. The shrink was always talking to me about did I feel suicidal. Was that it? I was going to kill myself with a little help from you and Jack. Oh my god, Michael. I never loved you, but... how could you hate me so much?"

Michael held her by both her arms now, very tightly. "I couldn't afford to loose my allies that were tied to me through your family. The only way to keep them and get rid of you, was for you to be dead. The kidnapping was a perfect opportunity for me to have it all, without being involved. I hadn't counted on them contacting your father. I just figured they'd kill you and that would be the end of it. Jack was an enterprising man. He went to your father, and got his price. Then he came to me. He figured there must have been a reason, I didn't pay the ransom. We made a deal. He failed and you made him loose all that money. He was not a happy man when he came out of the jungle. He came to me, again, and we hatched another plan. It was a matter of time before you killed yourself. So depressed."

"I won't die easily Michael."

"You may not have to. I didn't know about Amelio before. But now, you are much more valuable to me alive. I control you, you control Amelio... and I can manipulate the government here. It's a perfect set up."

"You slimy snake. I'm going to tell my father everything. I'm sure his friends at the State Department will be most interested in your plans. You'll be ruined."

"I don't think you'll be telling anyone anything." Michael's hand landed hard against Stephanie's face. The blow forced her to the wall. Stephanie had never seen Michael so intensely vicious. He had a temper, but it was usually under control. The only explanation Stephanie could find was that he had gone mad.

"You will do as you are told from now on and only as you are told." Michael landed another blow crushing her between the wall and his fist.

"We are married. You are my wife. You will never make me look foolish again." He hit her again and again.

"You will never again disobey me. I put up with you to this point for my career. In the States, I could not control you. I waited for the day we would be sent out of the country. I prayed for it. And it has come.'"

Michael was like an uncontrollable child, lashing out at her with his fists, wanting to crush her, hurt her the way he felt she'd been hurting him. He repeated over and over that she had made him look the fool, made him a laughing stock, jeopardized his career and this would be the last time she would do anything like that to him.

It was only too obvious to Stephanie that Michael was out of control. He might kill her. Stephanie found she was screaming, but it seemed hours passed before the door flew open. Rigby interceded and held Michael away from Stephanie, but not without great effort.

"If you don't stay in line Stephanie... I'll kill him... your lover. I'll kill him." The madman's words were wasted on Stephanie. Her ears could not hear his words.

Rigby forced Michael from the room, as Stephanie crumpled into a heap on the floor. Blood stained the carpet, where her face lay against it. Reality vanished and the sweet numbness of shock entered her body.

Chapter 8

In order to avoid a scandal, Stephanie was treated at the embassy rather than taken to the hospital. The press would have had a "field day" with this story. It was days before Stephanie could get out of bed without assistance. A nurse sat with her at all times. Stephanie had seen none of the embassy staff, since that night of insanity. The cook would leave the meals at the door and the nurse would see to everything. Stephanie was shocked to find that every time the nurse left the room, the door was locked. She asked the nurse about it and the nurse implied that it was for her own protection.

Stephanie wanted so badly to see Amelio... to have him hold her and make the hurt go away. Michael had threatened Amelio's life. Michael had nearly taken hers. Stephanie made many attempts to telephone her father, but Michael would not allow the calls to be put through. She tried to cable him and write him, but Michael intercepted all her attempts to contact her father. He was keeping her isolated from everyone. Was this her punishment for being a "bad little girl"? Would this incident set the stage for his future conduct toward her?

After nearly a week of "solitary confinement", Stephanie convinced the nurse to let her go downstairs. The nurse made a call to Rigby inquiring whether or not Mr. Cantrel were in the embassy and whether or not Mrs. Cantrel should be allowed downstairs. Michael was not in and permission was granted for Stephanie to come down. The nurse made Stephanie comfortable in the garden, then went to the kitchen to see about lunch.

Stephanie's lonely isolation was broken, when Sedro appeared in the garden with some small garden tools. Stephanie was overjoyed to see him. "Sedro ... I'm glad they found something for you."

"Senora..." Sedro looked curiously at Stephanie's bruised face. "What happened to you... another accident?"

Stephanie didn't answer the question, instead, she asked one. "Sedro, you are a brave young man, and very smart. Do you think, if I gave you a letter, you could find a way to deliver it for me... without anyone finding out?"

"Ah, si Senora. Sedro can do it.'"

"Good. I'll let you know when I have it ready."

Stephanie froze in her seat, as Michael appeared at the garden gate. He looked at her a long moment, then came toward her. Stephanie steeled her eyes on Michael, watching every movement trying to predict what he was going to do. With great tenacity, he ordered Sedro away, then took Stephanie's chin in his hand. He appeared to be controlled, but his eyes showed he was on the edge. He turned her face one way, and then the other. His eyes stayed cold, though not unemotional. The emotion was not regret, or sorrow, but rather ego and superiority. He felt he was in control. He was the master and she the slave. There relationship had always teetered on the master/slave arrangement... now it was clearly so. He expected her to be subservient ... to come at his beck and call. She was to be the beautiful little wind-up doll, to be removed from her box only for special occasions, to be shown off, never touched by others, and returned to her box lest his property be damaged.

190

"It doesn't look too bad. You should be sufficiently healed to attend the State dinner in two weeks."

Stephanie made a final appeal to Michael. "Michael... please let me go home... For the sake of your own sanity... let me go."

Michael's face twisted with anger, yet his voice remained calm. He took her hand in his and squeezed hard as he spoke. "I told you, we would not discuss this again. You will remain here with me. You are my wife and will remain so."

Michael stopped crushing her hand and left the garden. Stephanie felled her head into her hands and cried. It all seemed so hopelessly futile.

Over the course of several days, Stephanie found private moments to write a short letter to Amelio. She told him what was happening with Michael and explained that Michael had threatened his life... that Michael had intentions of using her to get to him. She asked that Amelio attempt to contact her father. Maybe he could get her out of Michael's hands. She sealed the envelope and tucked it into her pocket. This day, when the nurse escorted her to the garden, she found Sedro busy among the flowers. She sat near the boy and talked to him, until there were no eyes or ears to perceive them. She handed Sedro the letter and instructed him, where and to whom to deliver it.

Sedro stuffed the letter inside his shirt. "The president's house? You know some important people."

"Sedro, be very careful. If my husband were to find out..."

"He might hurt you again."

Stephanie was surprised at his remark. "How did you know?"

"Sedro is small. People do not notice him and talk freely."

"He might do worse than hurt me. He might hurt you. Here." Stephanie handed Sedro some money.

"No, Senora. You have already helped me to get this job. I owe you this favor."

191

Stephanie smiled at the boy, hoping, if she ever had a son, he would be as good of heart as this boy was.

Michael stayed clear of Stephanie. A week more passed and Stephanie had heard nothing from Amelio. There was no way of knowing whether or not the letter ever reached Amelio. Sedro had to give the letter to one of the staff at the president's home. The thought that someone might have intercepted the letter was a frightening one, but a very real possibility. Stephanie saw Amelio's picture in the newspaper. There was much speculation about an impending marriage, between Amelio and Elaina. Stephanie traced her finger over the outline of his face.

Michael dismissed the nurse and kept Stephanie a prisoner inside the embassy. She continued not to be allowed to go out, make any calls, or send any messages, unless Michael approved them. Michael had somehow convinced the staff that Stephanie was not to be trusted... a danger to herself. Only Rigby seemed to know what had really happened between her and Michael, and he wasn't talking. The staff watched her every move. They were tense and jumpy, as if they expected her to explode at any moment. Stephanie wasn't sure how much more of this she could take. Her own state of agitation was accelerating... she had to get out of there.

Midway through the second week, as Stephanie sat in the garden reading, Sedro tiptoed toward her. He slipped her a small envelope, then hurried away. Stephanie made sure no one was watching and opened the envelope, under cover of her open book. The note was short.

"Have arranged to get you out of the country. Be in the garden at midnight tonight, ready to travel.
Love, A."

Stephanie was flooded with relief. Finally, she would be out of this nightmare. She went to her room and packed a few things into a travel bag. Since she knew in advance she might be traveling by foot, she chose some appropriate clothes. She had no desire to relive her previous trip through the jungle. She had no idea how he might get her out of the country, but she was sure it wouldn't be through the airport in San Sabo. Tensely, she sat in the dark in her room waiting for the final hour. Every creek of the floor in the hall sent a chill through her body. Michael... was that Michael... would he find out?

Ten minutes to midnight. Stephanie still had not heard Michael come up to bed. Silently, she slipped from her room and down the stairs. She stole past the office where Michael was reading, the door partly open. Without a sound, she stepped through the French doors and out into the garden. A man appeared from behind a tree.

"Quickly."

"Who are you?" Stephanie whispered.

"Amelio sent me. Come, climb the rope over the wall."

With the man's help, Stephanie made the climb and jumped down to the other side where another man waited, impatiently.

The first man now jumped down from the wall and the two men pulled her down the street, into an alley. "We must wait here for the truck."

It was nearly 30 minutes before the truck rumbled down the street and stopped near the alley. The two men rushed her into the vehicle and they all sped off, out of the city. Neither man spoke to her or each other during the ride.

Dawn was breaking over the mountains when the truck ground to a halt. "We must make the remainder of the trip on foot, Senora."

Stephanie followed the men from the road into the ever increasing thickness of the jungle. They traveled all that day and half of the next until they came to a small village that seemed deserted. The men pushed Stephanie into one of the larger houses and told her to wait. The sky began to turn pink and orange as the sun sank below the mountains.

One of the men came to her and told her to sleep. Stephanie was exhausted. The thought of escape was the only thing that had kept her traveling at the hectic pace the men set. She was glad to be able to sleep, but unhappy that more time would pass, before she would be free.

They still were not leaving the next day. "Things are not yet ready, Senora. We must stay here until they are."

The man turned abruptly and she saw no one again that day. Stephanie became edgy. Three nights passed and the fourth was approaching. They still were not leaving.

Just as the twilight gave way to the moonlight, a figure appeared in the doorway. Stephanie did not recognize it as one of the men who had brought her there. When she did recognize the man, she came near to fainting.

"Hello, Stephie. Now... at long last... is our time." Jack walked to the table and lit the lamp.

Stephanie made a meager attempt at escape through the door, but Jack just pushed her back into the room.

"You gave me quite a whack on the head little lady. I must have been out at least an hour. Luckily I have a thick skull, or you might just have killed me. But you see, we were destined to meet again."

Jack made himself comfortable in a chair at the table.

"I watched you at the embassy, when you were in the compound and in the garden. I watched you in your bedroom, from the alleyway down the street. Your husband was even kind enough to let me into your bedroom. It was a hell of a temptation to take you right then and there... but I had my job to do. Then your husband changed his mind. Seems he had something better in mind for you. So... there I was again... not getting paid my full commission. A guy could starve around you. Luckily, the President called me to do another job for him. Seemed this American woman had captured little Amelio's heart and was a terrible threat to his government... an enemy of the State as it were. A message was sent by this American woman, asking Amelio to help her get away from her husband, who was keeping her a prisoner in the embassy. By the way, I was watching the night he beat you up. It was quite a show. Really got me worked up."

Stephanie was repulsed by his sickness.

"Anyway, the president intercepted the message the woman sent and devised a plan to be rid of her. He sent a message that Amelio would help her out of the country.

194

That's where I took over. I never collected a penny on you for all the work I did before. I told you I would collect... one way or another."

"But how will my death be explained?"

"You forget where you are. Deaths are easy to explain here. But you won't necessarily be dead, maybe you just disappeared. Mrs. Cantrel, as many people know, was very unsettled over what happened to her... Emotionally unstable. She was having an affair with a man... probably one of the men she met during those days she was missing. Her husband found out about it. He beat her badly... she ran away. You see, there are any number of possibilities for your death or disappearance. The president gets what he wants; his son will forget you, marry Elaina, make babies and create a whole royal family. He will never have to worry about you revealing his son as a kidnapper. Your husband of course, will probably be ruined... the president will discredit him and have him expelled from the country. He might try to implicate Amelio, but the fact that he is not a reputable man... beating his wife and keeping her locked up the way he did... his story will be dismissed."

"What do you get out of this, Jack?"

"You know I really like hearing you say my name." Jack smiled that lecherous smile Stephanie knew all too well. "I'll get a hundred thousand bucks... and you. Everyone gets something... even you. You get to be free of your husband. We will have a few days of fun. I'll be on my way and all your suffering will be over." Jack made it sound as if he were doing her a favor... a mercy. Jack stood up and moved toward her.

Stephanie refused to allow herself to lie down, like a sheep beset by a wolf. She picked up the stove iron and lifted it above her head, into a striking position, as Jack stepped toward her.

Jack laughed. "No. I won't let you hit me, again. I learned my lesson the last time. I won't underestimate you." Jack rubbed his head, where she'd hit him before. "I'll just sit here and wait." Jack went back to the chair and sat down. "You'll get sleepy, after awhile."

195

Stephanie backed into the corner and lowered the iron. She remained on the ready for any assault. He made a few threatening moves toward her, in jest, and laughed to see her react. He began to speak to her in a slow deliberate tone. He spoke to her of all the things he was going to do to her. His speech was obscene and perverse. Stephanie could feel herself flinch at his words, as if they were a physical strike against her. He went on and on, repeating the words louder and louder, then low almost in a whisper. He was playing his game with her again. Stephanie thought, if she could make him angry, cause him to loose control... that was the only way she had a chance at survival. Only if he wasn't thinking clearly, could she hope for some slight advantage.

She knew he had a temper and it could be provoked. She believed that his tolerance level was already lessened by the fact that she had beat him before. This would lessen his ability to keep himself under control... make getting to him easier... she hoped.

Not more than an hour had passed before Stephanie decided she had to try her plan. She took a deep breath, wet her lips and began talking to him. "You know Jack, you are a pitiful thing. Can you even get a girl without taking her against her will? Are you really that repulsive that you have to force a woman? Can you even perform, Jack, or are you just a big bluff? That's what it is, isn't it? You can't even finish what you start. Will you call someone else in to finish for you?"

Stephanie kept talking, prying the lid off his contained anger. Jack tried to ignore her remarks, but Stephanie could see the tension building in his face. He tried to drown out her words with his own. He shouted at her to shut up. Despite the fact that his logic told him what she was doing, his emotions were flowing hot.

Stephanie continued.

"It must be very depressing for you, knowing that you can never really have a woman... that you're not a real man."

As if propelled by a rocket, Jack was on his feet. The table between them flew across the room and shattered against the wall, clearing his path to her. Stephanie drew every drop of strength in her body to attention. She would only get one chance; if she failed... his eyes flashed wildly, his mouth snarled, and his body pulsed. His blood rushed hot through his veins, flushing his face.

The shot rang in Stephanie's ears, as if lightening had struck close by. Jack's expression changed and his body fell forward as if in slow motion.

Stephanie was not immediately aware of what had happened... not until Jack's body finally collided with the floor. She looked up toward the door, to find Amelio standing there, with the smoking revolver, still pointed at Jack. Jack never moved again.

Stephanie broke down into tears of relief, as Amelio held her tightly. Some other men rushed into the house speaking hurriedly in Spanish. Amelio took Stephanie outside, then lifted her into the jeep, and climbed behind the wheel. He pulled her close to him and lay her head on his shoulder.

"Everything will be all right, now. You sleep. We have a long ride."

When she woke, Stephanie was surprised to find herself back in San Sabo, at the president's home. Amelio carried her up the stairs to the room she had had the first time he brought her there. He lay her on the bed and kissed her, then kissed her again.

"Stephanie, I am so glad I got there in time. I don't know what I would have done, if I'd lost you."

"How did you know where to find me?"

Amelio smiled. "I didn't quite trust your husband. I just knew there was something wrong with him. I had no idea what, so I had him followed. I knew there was something wrong when he had a meeting with Jack Stodderd. I put a man on Jack, too. I found out what your husband had done to you. I visited the embassy, in hopes of seeing you, but he had you locked away. That young admirer of yours, Sedro, told me all that had happened. He told me of the note he had delivered, addressed to me. I never received it.

My father instead received it and used it against you. By the time I found out about my father's plans, you were already gone. Luckily, the man following Jack reported that he followed Jack to the village, where they were holding a woman. I knew it must be you. I was so afraid I would not reach you in time."

Amelio's smile grew. "It looked to me, though, that you were going to handle him pretty well yourself."

Stephanie's smile was a thoughtful one. "I don't know if I'd have survived, but Jack would never have forgotten me."

Stephanie turned to a more immediate subject. "What about your father, Amelio? What happens now?"

Amelio left the bed and walked to the window. He stared thoughtfully at the lawn below. "My father was killed two days ago. The remaining hold-outs from the old government bombed his car. They are all in custody and San Sabo is secure. The rest of the country is still experiencing skirmishes, but things will be under control before long. We have the support of the people and they are turning in any persons still speaking against us."

Amelio turned back toward Stephanie "I have been made acting president until we can safely hold an election... a fair election."

"I'm sorry about your father, Amelio. But I think the man replacing him is better suited to the post."

"Something happened to may father. He changed. He was corrupted. I still do not understand what happened. But that is behind us, We have our lives to get on with and a country to put in order."

Amelio returned to Stephanie and sat beside her on the bed. "I hope you will help me. There is so much to do. So much to get started. I'll need you beside me... to help me... keep me on the right path. With you looking over my shoulder, I think, I'll always make the right decisions."

"I think you would make the right decisions anyway. You haven't mentioned Michael. What of him?"

"You don't care for him do you?"

"No, Amelio. I don't care for him. I love you and I always will."

"Good. I have already sent for him. He will be here in a few hours. Do you wish to be present?"

"I think I should."

"Yes. I think he needs to see that he is finished, in your eyes, as well as in the eyes of my country."

Stephanie realized how dirty she was. "I think I need a bath before he comes."

"That's not a bad idea. Come on." Amelio took Stephanie by the arm, drawing her down the hall to the master suite. He flung open the doors onto a large sunken marble tub, already filled with steaming water. "See, I thought ahead and ordered it for you."

"Will you always take good care of me, Amelio?"

Amelio began to unbutton her shirt. "I will always and forever take care of you. I will be your lover... and your friend. I will be everything I can be to you... everything you will allow me to be to you." He pushed her shirt off her arms and dropped it to the floor.

"Amelio... I love you so much."

"I am glad we have that settled. Now finish undressing or do I throw you in as you are?"

The two of them laughed and played for over an hour. Then a knock came to the door. "Yes... What is it?"

"Ambassador Cantrel is here to see you, Mr. President."

"I want to make him sweat... make him suffer... wonder why I called him here... before I tell him he's through."

"Be careful, Amelio. I detect vengeance in your voice."

Amelio kissed Stephanie, "If I had my way Stephanie, if I were not the president and merely a man... his fate would be different."

Stephanie didn't have to ask what he meant, his eyes told her. What was the passion so intense in men that made them think of killing one another? Stephanie was glad to be a woman and have that passion alien to her.

Amelio entered the library with Stephanie on his arm. Michael was stunned and at first speechless to see Stephanie. He managed to speak, but his voice was shaky. "Stephanie... Where have you been?" His tone was scolding.

Amelio interjected. "Mr. Cantrel. Please sit down."

Michael sat, still staring in astonishment at Stephanie.

Amelio seated Stephanie in a chair across from Michael, then stood behind her, as he spoke. "Mr. Cantrel, your wife has charged that you physically and emotionally abused her, and held her captive against her will."

Michael began to squirm in his seat.

"There are allegations that you falsely secured monies for your wife's release and then deposited that money in a Swiss account. You further stand accused of attempting to buy a murder. And, lastly, there are charges that you intended to attempt to manipulate the government of this country. Is there anything you would like to say to these charges?"

Michael blustered. "What goes on between my wife and I is my business, not this country's. We are American citizens with diplomatic immunity."

"You have committed crimes while in this country. You are, to some extent, accountable for your actions. If it were wholly my decision, I would have you thrown in jail for the rest of your life. However, as a representative of a friendly country... no matter how bad a representative... and the fact that your wife has asked that I be lenient with you, you will be given an option. I can, of course, have you expelled. This would undoubtedly destroy any career you might have had and any future for one... if the reasons were made public."

"But you... you kidnapped my wife!"

"Merely propaganda spread by members of the ousted regime. No proof of any kind.. Now, as I was saying. I would be willing to allow you to resign your post here, for whatever reasons you might decide to give, in exchange for a... kindness."

Michael was grinding his teeth and throwing evil looks at Stephanie, as if this were all her fault. "What would this... kindness be?"

"You will return to your country, grant your wife an uncontested divorce, and agree never to return here... officially or unofficially."

It was painfully obvious to Michael, that he had no choice in this matter. He stood up and paced the room, running his hand through his hair.

"Mr. Cantrel... I want your answer."

"What choice have I? I agree."

"Good. Please arrange to be out of the country within 24 hours."

"And my wife? What about her?"

"Your wife has decided to remain here, as my guest. You may contact her, through your lawyers, and they may go through me."

Michael eyed Stephanie with a look of bemusement, at her having turned the tables on him so effectively.

"I guess I should have known there was enough of your grandfather in you, that you would not be beaten. He was a tough old man. He never liked my father or me. That's why I was so surprised, when you said you agreed to marry me... because he asked you to. He must have guessed you would eventually destroy me. I should have known he'd fulfill his threat to pay my family back. Goodbye, Stephanie."

Michael left like a whipped dog, with his tail tucked between his legs. Stephanie couldn't feel sorry for him anymore.

Stephanie and Amelio celebrated, quietly, that evening. Dinner was served on the balcony of the master suite. The moon was full and every star seemed out in celebration of their being together. They stood close on the balcony looking out over the countryside.

"Stephanie... I guess, I've never really come right out and asked you. So I will, now." Amelio took her hands in his and held his face close to hers. "Will you marry me?"

Stephanie smiled lovingly at him.. "Yes."

Amelio placed his arms around her and pulled her close. "Is there anything special you would like to do tomorrow? I feel like celebrating."

Stephanie laughed. "Anything but sky diving!"